MISSING PIECES

KATHRYN SCHLEICH

PUBLISH **HER**™

MISSING PIECES

© Copyright 2024 Kathryn Schleich

ISBN: 978-1-962457-19-4 (Hardcover)
ISBN: 978-1-962457-10-1 (Softcover)
ISBN: 978-1-962457-15-6 (E-book)
Printed in the United States of America
First Printing: 2024

Published by Publish Her, LLC
310 1/2 Main Street South
Stillwater, Minnesota 55082
www.publishherpress.com

Cover art by Kayla Franz

PUBLISH **HER**™

This book is dedicated to the hotel night manager and police officers who came to my aid after I experienced a life-changing episode of transient global amnesia.

JUNE 14, 2013, JUST AFTER MIDNIGHT

Jeanine Ramirez recognized the 30-something dark-haired woman approaching the front desk. She had been a Residence Inn guest for several weeks. She wore lavender pajamas and a summer robe, and a floral purse hung from her shoulder. She carried a large leather bag, its thick strap crosswise against her body, the bulk of it landing at her hip. It was the same Coach Rogue briefcase Jeanine's sister had, and she'd always admired it. The heaviness of the bag pulled the woman's shoulders into crooked misalignment. Jeanine couldn't recall the guest's name. She always seemed interested in Jeanine's life, asked about her family and her upcoming wedding in October.

The guest's name appeared in Jeanine's head in an instant: Madelyn Cummins. She breathed a sigh of relief. "Good evening, Ms. Cummins," she said, smiling. "How may I help you?"

Madelyn didn't respond with her usual pleasantries; instead she looked at Jeanine blankly. "I'm sorry to bother you," she said politely. "May I have a cup of coffee?" It was more formal than her usual outgoing nature.

"Certainly," Jeanine replied. "Regular or decaf?"

"Regular, please," Madelyn said.

"Cream or sugar?"

"Just black," Madelyn said, smiling faintly. "Thank you."

Something was not right. It was almost midnight. Jeanine had never encountered Madelyn at such a late hour. She appeared to be on her way out, but where could she be going in her pajamas? Jeanine decided she would get Madelyn a cup of coffee and ask if she needed help getting back to her room.

"I'll need to make a fresh pot, so it will take a few minutes," Jeanine said. "Is that all right?"

"That's fine," Madelyn said, her voice understanding.

Jeanine departed for the back room, emptied the coffee maker of its soggy dregs, added fragrant ground beans, and switched on the machine. It would take about five minutes for the coffee to brew—long enough for her to go back to the desk and check on the guest.

When she returned, Madelyn was seated on a sofa in the lobby, looking around as though she were seeing the hotel for the first time. The leather bag was on her lap. She'd left her floral purse and room key at the front desk.

The women's eyes met, and Madelyn nodded. Jeanine returned to the back room. The aroma of coffee filled her nostrils as the hiss of the brewing cycle completed. She poured the dark liquid into a paper cup and secured a plastic lid.

"Here you are—" Jeanine announced as she emerged from the back.

The lobby was empty. Madelyn's handbag and key sat unattended on the counter. Jeanine thought she may have gone to the restroom. Rather than waiting for Madelyn to return, she tucked the purse and key behind the desk and went to check the public restrooms. She opened the doors on both the women's and men's bathrooms, and they were dark. The automatic lights had not been activated.

It was possible Madelyn had a second room key and had gone back to her room. Perhaps she came downstairs unknowingly after taking a sleeping pill. Jeanine had heard stories about people taking Ambien and doing strange things in their sleep, like shopping and cooking. She told herself the unease she felt was premature.

She returned to the desk and typed Madelyn's name into the reservation system. She was staying in room 315. As Jeanine zipped the purse shut, she noticed Madelyn's cell phone was inside. She looped the strap on her shoulder, grabbed the cup of coffee and took the elevator to the third floor. Madelyn's studio was at the end of the corridor. She knocked on the door.

"Ms. Cummins? It's Jeanine from the front desk. You forgot your coffee and purse."

She listened for footsteps on the other side of the door, for the lock to unlatch. Silence. The heat of the coffee burned her fingers through the cardboard sleeve. Jeanine shifted the cup to her other hand and rapped harder.

"Ms. Cummins? Are you there?"

She pressed her ear to the metal door and listened for the faint sounds of movement. Still nothing.

Jeanine's master key card allowed her entry into any room. Although she hated entering a guest's room without their permission, she was concerned about Madelyn's welfare. She swiped the key card and the door clicked as it unlocked. She pushed the handle down and cracked the door. An overhead light in the room's entryway shined a golden triangle down to the carpeted floor. Jeanine felt a sliver of hope that Madelyn had been sleepwalking and made her way back to her bed where she was sound asleep.

"Ms. Cummins?" she called out.

Light glowed from the bathroom. Jeanine walked further into the studio. Rumpled sheets and blankets indicated Madelyn had been in bed at some point. At the small desk near the window, a laptop computer was closed, the charger plugged in, the workspace cleared. Jeanine recalled the briefcase slung across Madelyn's shoulder. Why had she taken the case with her and not her purse? In the bathroom, toiletries were arranged on the counter in an organized fashion. It appeared as though she had recently brushed her teeth.

Jeanine's thoughts raced. As a manager, she was trained on what to do when a guest was in distress. Was Madelyn in distress? She checked the hallways on the third level and headed to the elevator. She went to the second floor and checked the hallways there. Back in the elevator, on her way down to the first level, she prayed she'd find Madelyn in the lobby. It was unoccupied when she returned.

She checked her watch—it was 12:25 a.m. Per hotel protocol, she needed to wait 30 minutes before contacting law enforcement. Jeanine tucked the flowered handbag back behind the desk. She made a sweep of the first floor—the lounge, the hallways, stairwells, the areas that housed the ice and vending machines. She slipped outside and scanned the parking lot. There was no activity. It was a muggy summer night in Minnesota, almost eerily still. She heard the faint sound of traffic on Interstate 94 three blocks north.

At 12:40 a.m., Jeanine called 911 to report a hotel guest had gone missing. Within five minutes two officers appeared—a male and his female partner dressed in pressed dark uniforms.

"Her name is Madelyn Cummins. She's been staying here for several months. She came down to the front desk around midnight and asked for a cup of coffee, which I had to brew. When I returned to the desk, she was gone. She left this." Jeanine handed over the purse. "She's about 5-foot-7, pretty, dark brown shoulder-length hair. She was in her pajamas."

Lt. William Niles, a fit man in his early 40s, opened the handbag and removed the coordinating wallet. Madelyn's Minnesota driver's license showed through a clear plastic window. Thirty-six years old, 125 pounds, brown eyes. The name was familiar to him.

"Is this the woman you're referring to?" he asked, holding up the ID.

Jeanine nodded. "She has been staying at the hotel while her new home is being built. She's a lawyer. Divorce is her specialty, I think."

Lt. Niles' partner, Officer Amelia Wilcox, gave an affirming nod. "My cousin hired Cummins Law Office when she got divorced a year ago. She had great things to say about them."

She gestured for her partner to hand her the purse. "I'll run her license."

The lieutenant addressed Jeanine. "She came down to the desk just before midnight and asked you for coffee. Did she seem disoriented, under the influence of alcohol or narcotics? Bloodshot, watery eyes, slurred speech, trouble maintaining her balance—anything like that?"

"No. She was very polite, apologized for bothering me, and her speech was fine. She seemed a little distracted. I checked on her again while the coffee was brewing, and she'd taken a seat on the sofa with her briefcase. I planned to get her the coffee and ask if she needed help getting back to her room."

"You didn't see her again after checking on her? What time was that?"

"About 10 minutes after midnight. When I came back and saw the lobby was empty, I went to her room and knocked on the door. When there was no response, I let myself in. The lights were on, and the bed was unmade, but there was no sign of her. I checked floor by floor, thinking she may have gone to the wrong floor. I found nothing. The public restrooms and parking lot showed no signs of anyone. I hoped she would come back. It's like she vanished into thin air."

The building's automatic doors opened. Officer Wilcox handed her partner a slip of paper. "Ms. Cummins is the owner of the Mercedes E Class Coupe that's in the lot, brand-new, dealer tags still on it."

"She may have wandered off on foot," the lieutenant said.

"Seventeen more days," Maddie told herself.

She could hardly contain her mounting excitement, which was nearer to jubilation. In a few days, she would finally depart the Woodbury Residence Inn, where she had been living for months. The accommodations had not been shabby by any means. A well-lit studio, a pool and an exercise room, plenty of amenities—they had been a godsend after Maddie received multiple offers and sold her townhome less than 24 hours after it had been listed. But living in a hotel had worn itself thin.

She had chosen the studio because she thought she could reside in its cozy quarters temporarily. The 500 square feet of combined living and sleeping space with a kitchenette and bathroom had been adequate initially. She quickly discovered there was barely enough room for a few belongings and her limited wardrobe. Maddie couldn't fathom how people who traveled often for business survived out of a suitcase. She was anxious to be in her new home and spread out into a larger space.

Most of Maddie's waking hours were spent at her law office in historic downtown Stillwater. She had founded her solo practice nearly a decade ago, not long after she graduated law school. A short time later, she hired a seasoned paralegal, Simone Backstrom, who had quickly established herself as Maddie's right hand. As the firm's caseload of divorce and probate cases continued to grow, the office space had begun to feel cramped. Maddie hoped to expand the practice within the next year.

With no client meetings that required her presence in the office, Maddie was working from her room at the hotel. At the desk under the window, papers for a prominent divorce case were fanned out beside her laptop. Maddie looked up, took a deep breath and scanned the scene outside the hotel window. Beyond the parking lot, undeveloped fields sprouted tall prairie grasses, slopes and valleys of rusty brown soil, burgeoning trees in clusters. On the horizon were new homes under construction. In the not-too-distant future, residential neighborhoods would occupy this land.

Maddie contemplated the shifting narrative of the case. She was representing Jayne Koch, the third wife of Minnesota auto magnate Don Koch. It was six months into the divorce battle and the couple was still arguing over custody of their 3-year-old daughter, Gabby. Additionally, Jayne was certain Don was hiding marital assets. There was a prenuptial agreement, but now Don was claiming financial hardship, which meant Jayne would potentially receive far less in the divorce settlement than would otherwise be required by law.

Evolving criminal allegations were also complicating matters. During their marriage, Don had bet millions of their personal fortune, and borrowed $500 million more, to purchase a floundering rental car company. His intent was to salvage the company and sell it for a hefty profit, but he had grossly misjudged that the country would still be feeling the pinch of the 2008 financial crisis. Don was unable to turn the rental car company around, had lost millions, and filed for bankruptcy. His lender, Freedom Financial, was suing him for hundreds of millions in unpaid debt.

Despite his financial woes, Don continued to publicly flaunt his wealth. It angered his soon-to-be ex-wife, shocked his creditors, and stunned employees—many of whom had been laid off as Don drained the company of its assets and closed or sold the majority of its auto dealerships.

Don's alleged crimes were being investigated by Colin Towles, the trustee appointed to the bankruptcy filing in federal court, FBI agent Constance Lopez, and U.S. Attorney Paula Milton. Paula happened to be Maddie's best friend. Throughout the divorce investigation, Maddie had shared information she thought might be helpful to the federal case with the other women. There had been some recent developments, and Paula was on her way to the hotel to discuss them.

Maddie shifted her focus from the view outside to a copy of a Duluth News Tribune article on her desk. In a meeting with her client a week earlier, Jayne mentioned a failed golf resort in Duluth that Don had been a part of before they were married. Maddie's paralegal Simone had unearthed details about the project. She discovered the general contractor was Philip Lane of Lane Construction. Several months into the project, Philip had died in a single-vehicle accident on his way to the construction site near Lake Superior. Simone's investigation also led to details about how Don had initially funded the golf course project.

As Maddie reread the notes from the meeting with Jayne, there was a familiar tap-tap at the door. She opened it to her petite blonde friend balancing a cardboard tray of coffee, a small bakery bag and a blue leather tote.

"I thought caffeine and sugar were in order," Paula said.

"Bless you," Maddie said. She took the tray and bakery bag from her friend and placed them on the coffee table.

"I have officially hit an afternoon slump," Paula said. She released her tote to the floor as she sat on the mid-century patterned sofa.

"Me too," Maddie said. She took a sip of her latte.

"So tell me," Paula said. "What has super sleuth Simone discovered about Don Koch this time?"

"It appears he conned his first wife, Lisa Bennett, out of millions from a trust she received from her family before they got married. Simone reached out to her—we haven't heard back yet."

"Interesting," Paula said. She dug deep into her tote for a legal pad and pen.

"Lisa Bennett changed what was a single ownership trust to a joint ownership trust with her husband. Apparently, Don helped himself to more than $2 million dollars from the trust to finance a golf resort venture," Maddie said.

"This is the first I'm hearing about a golf resort," Paula said. "What happened?"

"It never materialized," Maddie said. She swiveled to grab

the Duluth News Tribune article from her desk and handed it to Paula.

"The general contractor died unexpectedly—" As she read the article, Paula's voice trailed off.

"The death was ruled suspicious, but the case ran cold," Maddie said.

"Definitely worth investigating further," Paula said.

"During my last meeting with Jayne, she said Don had stolen from her inheritance as well," Maddie said. "She's willing to testify."

"I'm listening," Paula said.

Maddie tapped at her laptop keys and turned the screen toward Paula. On it was an image of a white gold necklace with a large cushion-cut ruby hanging from a ribbon of intertwined pave diamonds.

"This is Jayne's great-grandmother's Cartier necklace, which Jayne's grandmother left her," Maddie said. "It appraised for a quarter of a million dollars at the time she inherited it."

"Stunning," Paula said. "It was stolen?"

"Jayne had it appraised again before she filed for divorce, and the appraiser discovered several of the gemstones had been replaced with fake stones. The only time the necklace was not in Jayne's possession was just after she and Don got married. Don was having several Rolex watches professionally cleaned and offered to take the necklace in to be cleaned as well. Jayne thought it was a good idea. Don returned the necklace to the safe in her dressing room a few weeks later. She didn't give it a second thought."

"Astounding," Paula said. "I'll share this information with Constance."

Maddie nodded. Both she and Paula had known Special Agent Constance Lopez for years. As a U.S. attorney, Paula had worked on a number of cases with her. They had become friends outside of work as well. The three of them had vacationed together the last few years in Isla Mujeres.

Maddie and Paula discussed the evidence for another hour or so, then caught up on their personal lives. They wrapped up their conversation as the descending summer sun became a blinding orb in the western sky.

"I'm going to dinner at that new restaurant, Longhorn Steakhouse," Maddie said. "Want to join me?"

"I would love to, but I've got an early morning yoga class," Paula said. "Let me know how the food is. Text me when you get back to your room."

"Will do," Maddie said.

JUNE 14, 2013, AFTER MIDNIGHT

The moon was full and luminous with an almost pink tint. Words flickered in Maddie's mind like a dying neon sign. "Strawberry moon" buzzed into her head and disappeared just as quickly.

She stumbled over jagged rocks protruding from the earth and fought not to fall. The heavy leather bag that hung diagonally across her body made her veer to one side and nearly topple over. With supreme effort she regained her footing. The sense she had lost her vehicle was overwhelming.

"Where is my car?" she wondered.

On the distant horizon, through the warm summer haze, lights seemed to hover against the dark sky. She had a brief flash of eating dinner at a restaurant.

"That's right," she recalled. "My car is in the restaurant parking lot."

The bag's strap pulled hard at Maddie's shoulder and cut into her abdomen. She yanked it over her head, and it fell to the ground with a thud. She rolled her stiff neck and squeezed her throbbing shoulder muscles. She didn't notice the stakes in the ground that marked this section of land for future development, or that she'd neglected to pick up her Coach briefcase. She methodically placed one bare foot in front of the other, trying not to slide down the incline. Her legs, arms and rear ached as if she'd already fallen multiple times.

New houses in various stages of construction rose behind her. She wandered onto the paved street and staggered back onto the dusty soil. She squinted at the scattered lights ahead—she was certain they would lead her to her car.

The ground sloped sharply. Tall reeds of grass bent in the breeze. Thick vegetation obscured partially buried boulders. She caught her foot on a rock and pitched headfirst toward the ground. Her arms flailed like a broken-winged bird trying to take flight. She fell forward hard, grasping at plants and earth and rocks as she slid on her abdomen down the hill and toward a massive tree. She took hold of a pitted rock, and her right shoulder twisted sharply as she came to a halt. The edges of the rock tore into fingers. She panted hard, spat dirt and blood.

Maddie remained prone until her breathing steadied. With her raw palms, she pushed herself up on all fours. She turned her head toward the pitted rock and froze in place—she was certain she saw teeth. She looked closer. In the bright light of the moon, she was sure it was not a rock. It was a skull. A human skull.

"Oh, god!" Maddie screamed.

Horrified, she crawled wildly away from the remains and toward the giant oak tree. On her knees, she surveyed the surrounding terrain. Thirty yards ahead, the hill was less steep. A path led up toward the construction site. Clouds floated over the moon and cast an eerie glow. Maddie questioned whether what she'd seen was real. She placed a hand on the trunk of the tree and steadied herself against it to stand. She turned toward the path and moved slowly up the hill.

If what she had seen was a skull, it must have been that of an animal, Maddie reasoned. She spotted level ground and continued to forge ahead. At the top of the hill, she turned and looked down. A person was standing in the exact place she was certain she'd seen the skull. She blinked hard to focus. The figure moved toward her. Her limbs began to shake uncontrollably. She sucked in a breath and began to run.

In the hotel lobby, Maddie's purse vibrated. Lt. Niles retrieved the iPhone from inside the bag.

"Hello," he answered.

"Oh, I'm sorry," the female caller said, startled. "I must have dialed the wrong number."

"Please, don't hang up," the lieutenant said. "Are you trying to reach Madelyn Cummins?"

"Who is this? Is Maddie OK?"

"Ma'am, this is Lt. William Niles with the Woodbury Police Department—"

"Oh my god, has something happened to Maddie?"

"How do you know Ms. Cummins?" he asked. He was polite, but firm.

"I'm—I'm Paula Milton, her best friend. Please, tell me what's wrong."

"When did you last see Ms. Cummins?" the lieutenant asked.

"Last night, around 8 o'clock."

"Can you come to the Residence Inn in Woodbury, Ms. Milton? Ms. Cummins has gone missing. We're about to start a search of the area. We'd like to ask you a few questions."

"I'll be there in 15 minutes."

* * *

Paula entered the hotel's lobby and looked anxiously toward the assemblage of police officers. Her fine-boned face showed no trace of make-up, and her hair was hastily tied back in a ponytail. She wore black yoga pants, a white T-shirt and sneakers. She paused, listening intently to the police officer she assumed she had spoken to earlier. He was describing search parameters.

"We believe Madelyn Cummins is on foot. She is approximately 5-foot-7, with brown shoulder-length hair. She is dressed in pajamas. Our initial search of the area will be two miles in each direction. Wilcox and I will head north, toward I-94."

Paula's heart pounded quickly as she approached the officer. "Sir, I believe we spoke on Maddie's phone. I'm Paula Milton."

"Thank you for coming," Lt. Niles said. "We're hoping you can shed some light on Ms. Cummins' state of mind."

"Maddie is a divorce attorney and I'm a U.S. attorney. We spent several hours discussing a case here at the hotel, in her room. We stopped working just before 8. Maddie was planning to have dinner at Longhorn Steakhouse and invited me to join her. I said no—I had planned to take a class early this morning— and asked her to let me know when she was back at the hotel."

Paula reached in her purse and retrieved her phone. She

opened the message app, scrolled through her messages and handed the phone to the lieutenant. "I texted several times before I went to bed and fell asleep." Her eyelashes were moist. "I should have gone to dinner with her."

Lt. Niles scrolled through a series of unanswered messages on Paula's phone:

"How was dinner?"

"Are you back at the hotel?"

"I hope you're not working! The Koch case will still be there tomorrow!"

"Going to bed. Call me!"

The texts covered a four-hour period.

"I woke up suddenly and realized I hadn't heard from her, and that's when I called and got you," Paula said.

"Were you concerned something had happened to Ms. Cummins?"

As Paula nodded, a strand of blonde hair came loose from her ponytail. She removed the hair tie and retied and tightened it. "Yes," she said. "It's not like Maddie to not respond to my texts."

"You mentioned the Koch case in one of your messages," Lt. Niles said.

"Maddie is representing Jayne Koch, the wife of Don Koch. You may have heard about it on the news."

Like most people in the Twin Cities, Lt. Niles was well aware of the Koch divorce. The Star Tribune and Pioneer Press newspapers had both carried stories on the implosion of Koch Automotive Group.

"Have you noticed any unusual behavior on the part of Ms. Cummins?"

Lines creased across Paula's forehead, and the pitch of her voice rose. "Like what, Lieutenant?"

Lt. Niles recounted the events Jeanine shared about Maddie coming to the front desk in her pajamas, asking for a cup of coffee, and leaving her purse with her wallet and phone on the counter.

As Paula considered all that Maddie had been through in the months leading up to now, her thoughts raced. "Maddie has been under an immense amount of stress," she said.

Sensing her growing anxiety, Lt. Niles suggested she sit on the sofa in the lobby. He signaled for his partner, Officer Wilcox, to accompany them. Paula sat and inhaled deeply as she organized events into chronological order in her mind.

"First, Maddie and her fiance broke up last year, which was completely unexpected," Paula said.

"What's her ex's name?" Lt. Niles asked.

"Michael Kelp."

Coincidentally, Lt. Niles and Michael Kelp played in the same recreational basketball league. At the recognition of the name, his face bore no emotions.

"Was the breakup amicable?" he asked.

Tears glistened in the corner of Paula's eyes.

"No. Michael confessed to having an affair and told her he was moving out. Maddie was devastated. She had no idea he was cheating."

Officer Wilcox jotted notes on a small pad. "What was the timing of it?"

"A year ago this month," Paula said, dabbing her eyes with a Kleenex she'd found in her purse. "Maddie decided to sell her town house and start fresh, to build the home she'd always wanted."

Lt. Niles nodded. "Did you notice any changes in her behavior?"

"Maddie was excited to leave the past where it belonged and start a new chapter," Paula said. "Her house sold the same day it went on the market. She is building her dream home. She also owns a law firm and has a full caseload. With the pressure of the Koch divorce case, I began to notice subtle changes. She seemed more anxious."

"How so?" Officer Wilcox asked, glancing up from her notes.

"I should have asked her if there was something I could do to help," Paula said. "She's my best friend. And now she's missing."

Lt. Niles placed a comforting hand on her shoulder. "Several police officers are searching the area," he said. "Can you describe how Ms. Cummins' behavior changed?"

"She was drinking more than usual. Not to excess. Instead of her usual two glasses of wine a couple of nights a week, she was drinking three or four. And more frequently."

"Does she take any medications?" Officer Wilcox asked.

"She was prescribed antidepressants after the breakup," Paula said, twisting the Kleenex.

"Any others?" the officer asked.

"She has taken anti-anxiety meds for years, since college. She used to have panic attacks, but she hasn't had one in a long time. When the Koch case began making headlines, she seemed more on edge."

"Any other medications?" Officer Wilcox asked.

The tissue was now twisted into a tight rope. "No," Paula said, her face forlorn. "I don't think she was abusing her medications, but they didn't seem to be helping. I just want her to be safe and sound."

Maddie ran for her life. The pursuer was gaining on her. Her heart pummeled against her breastbone. Sharp grass and spiky weeds tore at her bare feet and ankles. Up ahead, the vegetation gave way to a dirt lot. She strained to look beyond the clearing in search of a safe place. She continued to pump her arms furiously, just as she had running track as a teen. She didn't dare stop.

Something whizzed past her head. A bullet? Did her pursuer have a gun? The humidity pressed against Maddie's lungs as she sucked in large gulps of air. She imagined the running track at her high school and the 400-yard dash. She shifted her power from her arms, which had been doing most of the work, to her legs. In a competitive race there would be time for coasting too, but that wasn't an option now. The risk of being caught was a real possibility.

She glanced back over her shoulder. She did not see the figure that had been behind her, but she was certain she was still being followed. Her feet pounded against dirty pavement. She ran toward a group of homes under construction and into a two-story structure that was wrapped in Tyvek—the siding, doors and windows had not yet been installed.

Inside the house, she squatted in the corner of the front room. She was drenched in perspiration and struggled to regulate her heart rate and breathing. She clamped her hand over her mouth to muffle her panting and listened intently for footsteps on gravel. She thought she heard the sound of a shoe shuffling in the grit.

Headlights illuminated the road outside the front windows and beams of light angled inside the house. She scanned the space for a weapon of some sort to protect herself with. Swipes of light flashed along the walls and then disappeared. In the dark, her surroundings shape-shifted. She noticed lumber—2-by-4s and plywood—piled on the floor. She picked up a 3-foot scrap of wood and held the makeshift club in her hands. She was ready to fight.

Maddie began to count in her mind, "one-one-thousand, two-one-thousand, three-one-thousand," until she reached 300. Five minutes passed and then 10. She continued to listen for footsteps. Crickets chirped. Insects buzzed. An owl hooted from an unseen perch.

She made her way toward the garage and back outside, slowly and quietly. She looked around and saw no one. The flickering lights in the distance caught her eye once again. She had to get out of this place. She had to get back to her car.

JUNE 14, 2013, JUST BEFORE DAWN

Several members of the Woodbury Police Department, including Lt. Niles and his partner, Officer Wilcox, had been searching for Maddie for more than four hours. None of them had discovered any clues regarding her whereabouts, nor had they found anything out of the ordinary.

"Let's make one more pass through the new housing development," Lt. Niles said to his partner.

As he reached the intersection of an established and well-lit residential community, he turned the SUV around and headed back toward an area being expanded by the same real estate developer.

"Let's hope she's not—" Officer Wilcox paused, leaning toward the windshield. "Is that her?"

"Where?" the lieutenant asked.

"A block up in the middle of the street," she said, pointing. "There's someone walking."

Lt. Niles slowed the vehicle. The SUV's headlights outlined a single figure. It appeared to be a woman, and she seemed unaware a vehicle was behind her.

"I'm going to pull over and approach her on foot," Lt. Niles said. "We don't want to frighten her."

"I'll contact dispatch and let them know we've found a woman matching Madelyn Cummins' description," Officer Wilcox said.

Lt. Niles exited the vehicle and walked toward the woman. "Are you Madelyn Cummins?" he asked gently.

Startled, she turned and faced him. "How do you know my name?" she asked.

"Madelyn, my name is Lt. Niles," he said. He noted her swollen right eye and scratches, cuts and bruises on her face and arms. She was wearing tattered pajamas. "I'm from the Woodbury Police Department. We have been looking for you."

"Looking for me? Why were you looking for me?" she asked.

"You wandered away from the Residence Inn in the middle of the night. Do you remember leaving?"

Maddie stared blankly at the lieutenant. His partner slid out of the SUV and joined the two of them.

"Hello Madelyn, I'm Officer Wilcox. Do you know how you got here? Do you remember what happened?"

Maddie shook her head. The officer took Maddie's elbow, and she and Lt. Niles steadied and guided her to the SUV. Maddie winced as the officer helped her into the back seat of the vehicle and pulled the seatbelt across her.

"We're going to take you to the ER," the lieutenant said.

"Oh no, I don't need to go to the hospital," Maddie said.

"It looks like you've got some open wounds," Officer Wilcox said. "You need to be checked by a doctor, OK?"

"I need to get my car," Maddie said.

"Your Mercedes is in the parking lot of the Residence Inn," Lt. Niles said. "It's been there since last night."

"Since last night? What time is it?" Maddie asked.

"It's five o'clock in the morning, Ms. Cummins."

"That's not possible," Maddie said.

"It is," he said, pointing at the green LCD clock on the dashboard that read 5:07 a.m. "We've been searching for you quite some time."

Maddie slowly became cognizant of her surroundings. She was aware of the foul smell her body was emitting, too, and that her clothes were sticking to the vinyl seat beneath her.

"We're glad we found you, Ms. Cummins," Lt. Niles said, taking in her battered face in the review mirror. She looked as if she'd been severely beaten; it reminded him of the too many domestic violence calls he'd answered.

Officer Wilcox twisted her torso and spoke through the divider that separated the front and back seats. "We were concerned you may have been confused or disoriented and walked into traffic on I-94," she said.

"What?" Maddie said.

She stared at the officer in bewilderment. None of what either of them were telling her made any sense. Wandering away from the hotel? Walking into traffic? Why on earth would she do any of that? They must have been mistaken.

"People are worried about you," Lt. Niles said. "Especially your friend Paula."

Whatever was said next, Maddie didn't hear it. Curtains of

dense fog parted in her mind. On the stage, images of multiple scenes unfolded: the turbulent end of her relationship with her fiance, Michael; selling her home hours after she put it on the market; packing her belongings and putting them into storage; living in a hotel. As memories from the previous months came to her, she recalled nothing specific from the last few hours.

Then a flash of clarity: Her client, Jayne Koch, the estranged wife of auto dealer Don Koch. "I'm a divorce attorney," she said.

"Yes, that's right," the officer said.

"Where did you say you're taking me?"

"To the ER at Woodwinds Hospital. You need a physical exam. You may have been more seriously injured than you realize."

Maddie noticed how much her shoulder sockets hurt, as though they'd been wrenched out of joint. She looked down at her pajamas thick with grime, her arms and hands crusted with dried blood, her normally manicured nails chipped and broken. She wondered what exactly she'd been doing.

JUNE 14, 2013, 5:39 A.M.

Maddie wasn't fully aware she'd been asked to sit in a wheelchair outside the hospital entrance. She didn't notice the whoosh of the automatic emergency room doors opening or the gust of conditioned air as she was wheeled in. She didn't fully grasp the reason she was there. But as a woman called out her name and ran toward her, Maddie knew instantly it was her best friend, Paula.

"Oh my god, Maddie! I was scared to death!" Paula said, wrapping her arms around her friend in a gentle hug. "Where did they find you?"

Maddie shook her head. Her memory was blank.

"About a mile from the hotel, in a newer residential area," Lt. Niles said. "Let's get her checked in."

"I can help you here," a nurse in green scrubs motioned from behind glass.

Officer Wilcox wheeled Maddie toward the admittance desk.

Paula followed, handing Maddie her floral purse. "You left this on the desk at the Residence Inn," she said. "Your phone is in there, too."

Maddie recognized the handbag. She had no recollection of abandoning it.

Lt. Niles stepped aside. "We'll let you take it from here," he said to Paula.

"I cannot thank you enough. I was so afraid she—" Paula choked on her words.

The lieutenant removed a business card from his pocket and handed it to her. "Please let us know how she's doing. This is my direct number."

A second nurse stepped out from behind the desk to wheel Maddie to a bed. She was older, with hair that was short and muted red, which suited her. "Hi Madelyn, my name is Gwen Sorensen, I'm the head ER nurse."

"Can my friend come with me?" Maddie asked, gesturing toward Paula.

"Certainly," the nurse nodded.

She wheeled Maddie down a long tiled hallway with several curtained-off triage rooms. They stopped at a vacant room, where a standard-issue hospital gown lay folded on the bed. The nurse set the brakes on the wheelchair and helped Maddie stand.

"First thing I'll have you do is change out of your clothes and into this gown. I'll get you a warm blanket as well. I'll be right back." As she turned and closed the curtains swiftly, the metal rings rattled on the steel rod.

"Will you help me get undressed?" Maddie asked Paula. She removed her pajama top and then slipped off the bottoms, which were streaked with blood and mud.

"My god, Maddie," Paula said. "What happened?"

"I don't know." Maddie said. "But there isn't a part of me that doesn't hurt."

Paula held the gown open, and after Maddie slipped her arms into it, she tied it in the back. Nurse Sorensen reappeared with a blanket. Maddie sat, shifted her legs up onto the bed, and sank back onto the fluffy pillow. She realized her body was exhausted.

The nurse checked her vitals. Her blood pressure was low, her pulse slow. A second nurse, younger and brunette, informed Maddie she'd be assisting Nurse Sorenson. She typed Maddie's vitals into the computer.

Paula sat on the chair near the foot of the bed. "You'll feel better once you've had a hot shower," she said.

Nurse Sorensen gently examined Maddie's contusions. "You may have broken your nose. Do you recall falling?"

Maddie's face contorted as she tried to recall specific details. She knew only what others had told her. "I was at the Residence Inn and wandered away in the middle of the night," she said. "I have a faint recollection of standing in a field."

"Had you taken anything to help you sleep?" the nurse asked.

"No," Maddie said.

"Do you remember anything else?" Nurse Sorensen's expression was warm and concerned. "Maddie, I need to ask: Were you sexually assaulted?"

The horrific thought hadn't occurred to her. "No," she shook her throbbing head. "I'm not experiencing the kind of pain that would be caused by—" she struggled to get the word out. "Rape."

"Are you sure? If you're feeling any pain or discomfort in your genitals or rectum, we'll need to do a rape kit."

"I'm sure," Maddie said.

The nurse examined her arms, torso, legs and feet. "You have numerous lesions, some of which are quite deep. It looks like you fell multiple times. It appears you weren't wearing shoes. Do you recall what happened to your shoes?"

Maddie looked at her dirty, bloodied feet and shook her head. "I don't know," she said.

"We'll get your wounds cleaned and dressed," Nurse Sorenson said. She carefully examined Maddie's face. "How about your right eye? Is your vision OK?"

"The vision in my right eye is fuzzy. I can see out my left eye."

The assisting nurse continued typing notes at the keyboard.

"You are very banged up. The cuts and bruises will heal, but we need to be sure your nose isn't broken. The doctor will want an X-ray of your face and possibly your entire head."

"OK," Maddie said.

"Are you on any medications?" Nurse Sorenson asked.

"Yes, I've been on anti-anxiety medication for most of my adult life," Maddie said. "I recently started taking something for depression."

"Did you use recreational drugs? Had you been drinking alcohol?" the nurse asked.

"No," Maddie said.

"Did you have anything to drink at dinner? At the steakhouse?" Paula asked.

A memory came to Maddie in a flash. "That's right, I went to Longhorn Steakhouse. I ordered the filet mignon, mashed potatoes and asparagus." She was thrilled with this new revelation. "I had two glasses of riesling."

"You're positive you only drank two glasses of wine?" Paula prodded.

The question irritated Maddie. Then she recalled a recent happy hour at the hotel bar, ordering a third cocktail to take the edge off, and the look on her best friend's face as she suggested they call it a night. Paula expressed concern that evening that Maddie had been drinking more than usual.

"I distinctly recall ordering two glasses of riesling—one before, and one with dinner," Maddie said confidently. "I remember deciding against dessert and asking for the check."

"For the record, I don't think you have a problem with alcohol. I worry about you mixing alcohol with your medications." Paula paused and took Maddie's hand. "You've been through a hell of a lot this past year."

Tears spilled down Maddie's face, stinging the abrasions on her cheeks. "I have been mindful of my drinking since we had our talk," she said.

Nurse Sorensen offered Maddie a box of tissues.

The curtains of the triage area opened. An attractive dark-haired physician entered. "Hi Madelyn, I'm Dr. Elaine Englund. I've been told you went for a midnight stroll."

Maddie appreciated the doctor's light-hearted nature, which instantly put her at ease. "Yes, but I don't seem to recall much of it."

"I've ordered a CT scan of your head," Dr. Englund said. "We'll check for broken bones, especially your nose. We also need to confirm you don't have a traumatic brain injury. Nurse Sorensen will bring you down for the scan and I'll be back once we have the results."

In the CT imaging room, a round-faced radiologic technician introduced herself to Maddie and explained the steps of the procedure. Nurse Sorensen helped Maddie onto the table. Her battered body made it difficult for her to get comfortable lying down on the rigid platform.

"How long will the CT scan take?" she asked.

"Just a few seconds," the tech said. "You're not claustro-phobic, are you?"

"No," Maddie said, thankful the process wouldn't take long.

Inside the tube, Maddie's trepidation began to rise. What if her memory loss was caused by a brain tumor or cancer? She fought back tears thinking of her mother's untimely death to breast cancer. What if it was a sign of early onset Alzheimer's or dementia? Her paternal grandfather had succumbed to dementia, and the slow degeneration of a vibrant man reduced to a shell of a person had been heartbreaking to witness. She did her best to force the anxious thoughts aside and concentrate on the technician's instructions.

Once Maddie was back in her bed in the ER, Paula took notice of her friend's increasing nervousness. Paula used the remote to raise the head of the bed and helped Maddie get more comfortable. She distracted her with small talk until the scan results came in. It didn't take long for Dr. Englund to return through the curtains.

"Everything is normal on the CT scan," she said, her expression pleased as she stood at the side of Maddie's bed. "You'll also be relieved to know you did not break your nose."

"What about the memory loss?" Maddie asked.

"It appears you've experienced an episode of transient global amnesia, or TGA. It's a condition that is precipitated by stressful life events," the doctor explained.

"Like ending a long-term relationship, selling a house, building a new home, and working on a high-profile legal case?" Paula asked, her tone facetious.

"Certainly, those kinds of events rank high, right next to the death of a loved one," Dr. Englund said. "Generally, TGA episodes last up to 12 hours, and in rare cases symptoms can persist for 24 hours. Most patients don't have a recurrence."

Maddie sat up straighter, both thankful and apprehensive in the same moment. "When will memories of what happened— why I left the hotel, where I was, what I did for hours— come back?"

Dr. Englund smiled empathetically. "It's not likely your memories will come back."

"Not knowing what happened is so strange," Maddie said. "I'm feeling something I can't really explain. Like grief."

"Those feelings are to be expected. You are mourning a part of your life that's been lost to you. Those who experience TGA rarely recall what happened leading up to the episode. Occasionally, however, some memories return."

"Are you saying her memory has been erased?" Paula asked.

"Essentially, yes," the physician acknowledged. "You are alert, coherent and making sense, all positive signs. However, it hasn't been 12 hours since you left your hotel. So even with your CT scan being normal, I'd like to admit you overnight for observation."

"That's not necessary," Maddie protested. Since the tests showed nothing serious, a hospital stay seemed unwarranted. "I am stiff and sore, but I'll be fine. I have meetings today."

"We can't hold you against your will," Dr. Englund said. "But you have suffered a severe trauma and it's best to err on the side of caution."

Paula reached into her tote bag, took out a compact mirror, opened it and handed it to her friend. Maddie looked at herself for the first time under the stark, fluorescent hospital lights. She gasped at the scratches and angry welts of pink and red flesh staring back at her. Crescents of dark blood pooled under both eyes. Her right eye was swollen like a boxer who'd been on the losing end of a fight. Her hair was a stringy, matted mess.

"We need to attend to your injuries. Once you're cleaned up, we may see that some are more severe than we initially thought," Dr. Englund said, folding her arms. "I strongly recommend you take at least a week to recuperate. No working, physical exertion or undue stress. Your body will feel more sore and stiff tomorrow. You need to rest and heal."

"You've experienced a medical emergency, Maddie," Paula said sharply. "I will call Simone and have her cancel your appointments for the week. I'll collect your belongings from the hotel and check you out. Once you're released from the hospital, you'll stay with me."

Selfless acts like this made the two women as close as sisters—always looking out for one another, celebrating accomplishments, overcoming setbacks, encouraging each other's growth. They had both experienced their share of adversity, and each had discovered an innate resilience. In law school, their bond of love and respect for one another had knitted into an unbreakable bond. Maddie looked at Paula's bright blue eyes and felt extreme gratitude.

Maddie was patched up and admitted. Hospital beds were limited, so she was placed in the maternity ward. She couldn't wait to take a shower. With Paula nearby to steady her, Maddie stepped under a soothing cascade of warm water. She shampooed her hair twice and gently washed off the grime and foul odor. The water cleansed away the fog, invigorated her body and lifted her spirits. She changed into a fresh gown and towel-dried her hair as she sat on the edge of the hospital bed.

"Would you like to keep these?" Paula asked, holding the plastic bag the hospital had provided for Maddie's soiled clothing.

"No, throw them out," Maddie said, shaking her damp head adamantly. "I never want to see them again."

M addie's sleep was agitated. The starched sheets of the narrow hospital bed and her tender muscles made finding a restful position difficult. Her mind hovered between light slumber and edgy wakefulness. She wanted desperately to reconstruct the events that had ensued during those missing hours.

The recollection of being in an open field, the discovery of a human skull and someone chasing her loomed, but everything was out of focus. She wondered if it was all a dream. None of it seemed logical or plausible. What was she doing in a field? Why would human remains be buried there? Who would have followed her?

As a new day dawned, Maddie decided none of it was true. The bones—if that's what they were—belonged to a wild animal, or someone's deceased pet. She had constructed absurd scenarios in her imagination as a lingering effect of the amnesia. Her mind wasn't quite right.

That afternoon, as she sat in the recliner in her hospital room and waited to be released, Maddie still couldn't grasp why she'd left the hotel in the first place. And there was something else pricking at her brain. Something about the Koch divorce case and Don Koch's businesses. She couldn't recall what it was specifically, but she remembered discussing the case with Paula. She recalled feeling uneasy about some of the details they discussed. She squeezed her eyes shut and tried to remember why exactly she felt that way. Nothing.

She pounded her fists on the arms of the blue vinyl chair. She had no patience for the possibility her memories might reappear gradually. She wanted her mind to be exactly the way it had been—logical, decisive, keen—and she wanted it now.

At Paula's two-story town house, Maddie found the lower-level guest bedroom had been comfortably made up for her. Paula had unpacked her belongings, hung up her clothes and organized her shoes.

"You did not have to do all this!" Maddie exclaimed. "You've done more than I could ask for." She squeezed her friend's shoulder.

"I am happy to have you here," Paula replied. "You've done the same for me. In case you don't already know, you're staying as long as it takes for you to heal and finish the house. The fridge is stocked with your favorite fruit, veggies and yogurt. Simone is going to reschedule your clients. I'll be at my office all day. In the meantime, you rest!"

Maddie followed Paula up the steps, noting the acute heaviness in her legs as she climbed, and the soreness in her right shoulder. A new thought occurred as she entered Paula's immaculate white kitchen. "Where are my briefcase and files? I promise I won't do any work; I just want to get organized."

CHAPTER EIGHT

"I've been meaning to ask you about that," Paula said. "I didn't see it when I packed up your hotel room. Did you leave it in your car?"

Maddie shrugged. "Given everything that's happened, I'm not even sure where my car is."

"That I can help you with. Simone and I will be picking it up from the hotel parking lot today. Don't worry, I'm sure your bag and files are in there. I'll need your key fob."

Maddie's floral purse sat on the light gray patterned quartz counter. She located the fob inside and handed it to Paula. "I'm sure you're right. I'll put it out of my mind. My plan is to catch up on 'Judge Judy' for mindless entertainment. Perhaps 'Jeopardy' to make certain my brain cells are still functioning."

"Great plan," Paula said.

Maddie exhaled. "There is one important task I will accomplish today," she said. "I'm going to write thank you notes to the Woodbury Police Department and the Residence Inn."

* * *

Paula arrived home at twilight bearing gifts of delicious food: spinach salads crowned with succulent salmon, French bread, chocolate cupcakes.

"Smells wonderful," Maddie said. She rose from the sofa and set place mats, plates, napkins and silverware on the kitchen island. "What would you like to drink?"

"Iced tea for me. There's a pitcher of it in the fridge."

Maddie pulled two tall glasses from the cabinet and filled them with ice and tea.

"Your briefcase wasn't in the car," Paula said, as she took a seat on a high-top chair at the island. "I went back to the front desk one last time. Jeanine Ramirez was there, and I asked if she'd seen it. She said you were wearing it diagonally across your body when you came down and asked for coffee."

Maddie took a bite of warm salmon and spinach. If she had carried the heavy leather case with her, it could explain her sore shoulder. Had she lost it along the way? The Koch divorce files, and several cases were organized in that bag. Private conversations protected under attorney-client privilege. Her panic rose. "Shit," Maddie said.

"Do you remember where you last had it?" Paula asked.

Maddie closed her eyes and tried to visualize where she may have left it. She saw grassy terrain, wild brush. Suddenly, she remembered the case's strap cutting into her shoulder, the weight of it pulling her down, nearly causing her to fall.

"I think I was in a field," she said and sighed. "I have no idea where that might be."

G raphic nightmares continued to disrupt Maddie's sleep. In the dark, she slid down a steep hill, and grabbed at whatever she could to halt her descent—vegetation, soil, rocks. Under a flash of light from the full moon, the object she'd finally taken hold of became visible—the lower jaw of a human skull. She stumbled to get out of there. A faceless figure appeared behind her. She ran as fast as she could, tried to escape whoever it was. She sought cover in a dilapidated building.

"Help! Help!" Her own panicked voice woke her.

Paula heard Maddie call out and ran to the guest room. She switched on the lamp on the bedside table. "You're safe, Maddie, I'm here," Paula said, sitting on the edge of the bed.

Maddie's whole body shook. Her pajamas were soaked in sweat. "There were bones—" Maddie said, her voice filled with terror.

"It was a nightmare," Paula said. "A bad dream. Tell me about the dream. What do you remember?"

"A field. A steep hill. A big tree. I was sliding and had to stop myself before I crashed into the tree. I grabbed a—" Maddie lifted her hand and examined the gashes in her fingers. She showed the marks to Paula. "A skull, half buried in the dirt. A human skull. With teeth."

"Maddie, I think you are remembering something that really happened," Paula said.

"The ER doctor said—"

"She said most victims of TGA don't recall what occurred leading up to the episode. But what if you are?"

"Oh my god," Maddie said. "What happened to me?"

"I think something traumatic happened. I think you witnessed or discovered something so horrible that you are blocking out the memory. Your subconscious is revealing what happened. You need to write it down," Paula said.

The thought of reliving those moments petrified Maddie. She knew there was more to this story, but could she uncover those missing pieces?

"OK," she reluctantly agreed.

"I'm so sorry you're going through this," Paula said, hugging her friend.

"I'll never fall back to sleep," Maddie said. She flipped aside the blankets and wrapped herself in her robe. "I'm going to write this down before I forget."

"I'll make us some coffee," Paula said. "I won't fall back to sleep either."

Upstairs Maddie settled at the dining room table with a legal pad and pen. The words came sporadically, tiny details cracking through the heavy wall that encircled her memories and protected her from the reality of the trauma she had endured.

A violent nightmare came the following night as well, and

Maddie's guttural cries woke both women once more. She was in an abandoned building, hiding from someone. Was it a commercial property? A house? Who was she hiding from? She cowered in the dark in terror as footsteps from her pursuer drew near.

Maddie wrote it down. Paula encouraged her to keep writing, to focus on sensory details, anything that might elicit more memories. When Maddie read what she'd written, she doubted any of it had happened. Her notes looked like the scrawling of a madwoman. Still, something pushed her to keep going, to keep searching for the truth.

* * *

"I'll start with the latest on Don Koch," Maddie's paralegal, Simone, said over the phone. "He was arrested this morning for nonpayment of alimony to his first and second wives. He's been taken to the Hennepin County Jail. There's a family court hearing at 2 o'clock. He's been dodging questions about his finances and Judge Syverson is losing patience."

"Don failing to meet alimony obligations will make headlines," Maddie said. "We need to be at the hearing."

"My thoughts exactly. I'll swing by Paula's and pick you up at 1 o'clock," Simone said.

Maddie felt a rush of adrenaline as the details of the Koch divorce case came to her. She knew her firm represented Jayne Koch, Don's third wife. She recalled the circumstances of the divorce settlement of Don and his second wife, Tiffany, and in particular, the highly unusual permanent alimony, which rarely happened in marriages of fewer than 20 years. He and Tiffany were married just over a decade. Their relationship started when she was 19 and worked as the receptionist at the Koch Automotive Group headquarters. They wed when she was pregnant with their first child and had a second child four years later.

As the details of the case resurfaced, Maddie realized she recalled little about Don's first wife, other than her name—Lisa Bennett.

"I have an update on Lisa Bennett's trust fund," Simone said, as if on cue.

"Her trust fund?" Maddie asked, confused.

"We discussed it the day before your TGA episode," Simone reminded her. "Somehow Don convinced his first wife, Lisa, to make him a joint trustee on her trust fund, which held over $3 million. He claims she knowingly invested $2 million in a golf resort. Apparently, the development went south fast. Don claimed he was the victim of an unscrupulous general contractor, and the money was gone."

Maddie sat motionless as a memory about the case flittered in the corner of her mind. She closed her eyes and searched for it.

"Maddie? Are you still there?" Simone asked.

"Yes, sorry. Did Lisa Bennett sue for damages?" Maddie asked, hoping her random recollection that Lisa hadn't sued Don would be confirmed.

"No, she did not," Simone replied. "She was awarded

alimony, but not nearly enough to make up for what Don bilked from her trust. There's no record of litigation."

The doorbell at Paula's town house chimed.

"Hold on for a sec, Simone," Maddie said. "Someone's at the door."

Each step she took toward the front door was slow and labored. She squinted to focus on the outline of a figure outside the lead glass on the door. It stopped her in her tracks. It was Michael Kelp, her former fiance.

"Simone, I'm going to have to call you back," Maddie said, the pitch of her voice noticeably higher.

"Everything OK, honey?" Simone asked.

"Yes. I'll call you in 15 minutes."

M addie cracked the door less than halfway, not bothering to disguise her annoyance.

"What the hell are you doing here?"

The cut of his gray custom suit fit well over Michael's tall, muscular frame. His thick brown hair was combed back and tapered along the edges. The expression on his face was concerned.

"Good morning, Maddie," he said, pressing a palm against the door. In the other hand, he held a latte. "I heard what happened and I wanted to see if you were all right."

"What do you mean you heard what happened?" she snapped.

"Please, may I come in?" he asked gently. "I brought you a latte."

She reluctantly stepped back. Michael entered and closed the door behind him. Perspiration glistened on his forehead. As they stood awkwardly in the entryway, he tried not to stare at the contusions on her face. Maddie wondered if it was contrition she saw in his sculpted features.

"Can we sit for a minute?" he asked, holding out the coffee.

"No, thank you," she said. "How did you hear about me?"

"Bill Niles, the Woodbury police officer who—"

"What the fuck?" she interrupted.

"Bill and I have played in a rec basketball league for years," he said.

That meant Lt. Niles knew Michael when he and Maddie were still a couple and planned to get married. It meant they had been friends when Michael decided to shatter Maddie's heart and cheat on her with Elizabeth Mann, a Hennepin County district attorney he worked with. Michael may have even confided in Lt. Niles about his betrayal. Humiliation and resentment flushed hot on her cheeks.

"What are you really doing here?" she asked.

"Bill said you were in rough shape when they found you," Michael said. "I wanted to make sure you were OK."

"You got what you came for," Maddie said.

"You're OK?" Michael asked. "Bill said you were missing for hours."

"I'm fine. The scrapes and bruises will heal."

"Maddie, I was—"

"Jesus Christ, Michael," she said, throwing her hands up. "Why do you care?"

"Because I—" His voice was soft and deliberate. "I love you, Maddie."

It was not what she wanted to hear. "How dare you," she said, flinging the door open. Steamy summer air filled the entryway. "Please leave."

"Maddie, I mean it. I've always loved—"

"You've always loved me? You have a strange way of

showing it. You demeaned me. I won't allow that to happen again. Ever."

"I made a horrible mistake. Elizabeth and I split up. I broke off the engagement," he said.

"I don't care," Maddie said, resolute. "I have moved on."

Michael exhaled a long breath. "Maddie, I want—"

"I don't care what you want," she said, cutting him off. "I want you to leave."

An uncomfortable silence hung between them.

"OK," he said finally and reached for the doorknob. "Before I go, there's something important you should know about Don Koch." He turned back toward Maddie.

"What makes you think I've missed any crucial details regarding the Koch case?" she asked.

"This is not public knowledge yet," Michael said. "He was arrested an hour ago for failing to pay alimony to his first and second wives. There's a hearing scheduled in family court this afternoon."

"You remember Simone, my supremely skilled paralegal? She does more before the sun rises than most people do all day. Despite the information not being public, she shared those very same details during our morning brief," Maddie chided.

Michael paused. "Did she also share that Elizabeth left the Hennepin County District Attorney's office to work for Gold and Stein, the firm just retained by Don Koch to represent him in both the divorce and his criminal case?"

"So what?" Maddie said.

"Elizabeth is Don's divorce attorney," Michael said.

"Don Koch has an army of attorneys on his payroll. Elizabeth is just another foot soldier."

"Before we broke up, Elizabeth mentioned that one of her new clients was hell-bent on taking his divorce case to court," Michael said.

"That sounds a lot like a breach of attorney-client privilege to me," Maddie said.

"She didn't say who the client was; I presumed she meant Don," Michael said.

Maddie did not let on, but the information caught her off guard. The possibility of the Koch divorce going to court was the worst-case scenario. It meant an already dragging case could be drawn out even longer. She kicked herself for not considering the possibility.

"He'd be a fool to prolong another divorce," Maggie said, grimacing as she shifted her weight from one foot to the other.

"Do you want to sit?" Michael asked, noticing her discomfort.

"I'm fine," Maddie said. "If Don Koch takes his third wife to court after failing to pay his first and second wives, the media will crucify him. Why would his legal team allow that?"

"I don't know," Michael said. "I do know his monetary problems are much bigger than he's letting on. Most of the people helping him have been doing so to save their own asses. I suspect that will change."

"Hmm," was all Maddie could think to say as her thoughts spun.

"Maddie, Don Koch is a dangerous man. He'll use any

means necessary to make his legal problems disappear. Please be careful."

"Thanks for the concern," she said.

"Maddie," Michael said softly. "I am truly sorry for the pain I caused you."

"I appreciate the information," she said cordially and held out her hand. "All the best to you."

"You, too," he said.

To her dismay, the exchange with Michael fatigued Maddie. She wanted nothing more than to be back at full strength and resume her normal routine. The thought of having to wait for her body and mind to return to 100 percent was maddening. She often counseled her clients to practice patience during divorce proceedings. Now, in her own life, especially when it came to figuring out the puzzle of TGA, patience was not one of Maddie's virtues.

Simone stopped by Paula's to pick up Maddie and drove the two of them downtown to the Hennepin County Family Justice Center. The concrete and skyscrapers in the bustling city held the summer heat and raised the temperature to nearly 100 degrees. The architectural style of the Family Justice Center was referred to as modernism, but there was nothing new about the squat six-story building—it was just another drab government structure.

The lines for the metal detectors in the lobby were slow. The family court system was always busy. Maddie and Simone found two seats at the back of the wood paneled room mere minutes before the appointed hour. At the front of the courtroom, at opposing tables, Don Koch and his second wife, Tiffany, were seated with their attorneys. In the row of chairs directly behind Tiffany's table, Don's first wife, Lisa Bennett, sat next to her attorney.

The differences between Tiffany and Lisa were noticeable, even from the back of the courtroom. Tiffany's platinum blonde hair was fried from overprocessing. Years of sun worshipping had taken a toll on her skin. Deep lines punctuated her mouth and eyes, making her appear much older than mid-30s. She wore an ill-fitting print wrap dress that accentuated her large breasts. Her strappy silver sandals were a bold choice for the courtroom.

Though she was in her 50s, Lisa, who was fair-skinned and wore almost no makeup, appeared much younger. She wasn't slender, leggy or blonde, like the women Don married after her. She was attractive, classy. Her light brown chin-length bob was perfectly styled with caramel highlights that framed her face and appeared natural. She wore a crisp navy blue pantsuit and nude pumps.

While the women waited quietly with their counsel, Don leaned back in his chair, a smirk on his face as he chatted with his attorneys. His slick head of receding gray hair was in need of a good cut. Unlike Tiffany's sun lamp tan, Don's was spray-on orange. His suit was expensive and tailored, but it wasn't custom. He donned a pale blue and white striped Winchester shirt with a white collar and wide cuffs, and a geometric patterned silk necktie. The shirt and tie cost a pretty penny at one time, but they reeked of another decade. His look was reminiscent of Gordon Gekko's garb in the '80s movie "Wall Street."

Elizabeth was one of the two attorneys representing Don. As Don spoke to her, she smiled and nodded her lustrous head of flaxen hair.

A bailiff announced, "All rise! The Court of the 10th Judicial Circuit Family Division is now in session, the Honorable Judge Kathleen Syverson presiding."

Judge Syverson wore her gray-blonde hair short and carried her medium build with dignity. She was widely regarded as a fair-minded and compassionate magistrate.

Her voice was calm yet forceful. She did not mince words. "Mr. Koch, we are here today to discuss your not meeting the terms of your alimony agreements, but we cannot do that without considering your myriad of other legal problems. At the heart of those problems is your bankruptcy and the question of where your funds have gone. And also, where your money is coming from. You continue to claim financial hardship, but by all appearances, you are living a comfortable life."

"Your Honor," Don broke in, "My former attorney advised me to liquidate my 401(k) and talked me into filing bankruptcy. As a result, I have had many unexpected financial obligations."

"Mr. Koch," the judge said, reviewing the papers on her desk, "when you testified in bankruptcy court, you stated you did not consult an attorney prior to cashing out your retirement account. As far as the bankruptcy filing, the decision was ultimately yours. Unfortunately, your former attorney's untimely death means we cannot hear from him on this matter."

"I had nothing to do with—"

He was interrupted by the second attorney at his table, an

impeccably attired older gentleman who placed a firm hand on Don's shoulder as he stood. "Your Honor, Bernard Gold here," he said. "If I may, I'd like to address the matter of Mr. Koch's representation."

The judge nodded. "You may."

"Don Koch's former attorney's unexpected passing was unfortunate. My firm, Gold and Stein, is now handling both the divorce litigation and criminal representation for Mr. Koch."

"Thank you, Mr. Gold," Judge Syverson said. "Your presence here begs the question: How does someone experiencing financial hardship retain a firm such as yours?"

Don's first wife cleared her throat.

Simone nudged Maddie. "That's Lisa Bennett," she whispered. "After the hearing, let's see if she's willing to meet." Maddie agreed.

Bernard did not respond to the judge's question—he knew it was rhetorical. Bernard Gold was easily recognizable from multiple billboards throughout the Twin Cities and frequent appearances on the TV news. As a criminal lawyer, he was considered one of the best. He was also known to be one of the most expensive.

"I'd like to hear from your client about his spending," Judge Syverson said. "Mr. Koch, where is your money coming from, and where is it going?"

Bernard took his seat.

"I am doing some consulting work, but the money I make is not enough to cover my expenses," Don explained. "As I mentioned, I have many financial obligations."

"Alimony is one of those financial obligations," the judge scolded. She selected one of the documents from the stack in front of her. It noted that at the time Don and Tiffany's divorce was granted, permanent spousal maintenance was awarded to Tiffany, and child support was awarded for their two children, now ages 16 and 12.

"I always take care of my kids," Don said. "This has been really hard on them. When a reporter on last night's news said I might go to jail, they turned to me with tears in their eyes and made me promise that would never happen."

As Don wiped an invisible tear, Tiffany shook her head. Lisa looked down at her hands, which were folded in her lap. Also not buying his act, the judge continued to read through case documents.

"Mr. Koch, from what I can tell, you have the means to fulfill the terms of the alimony agreements, yet your payment history has been sporadic. You have a reputation for coming forward in the 11th hour to satisfy the court's order and avoid jail time. I wonder if incarceration will force you to take your financial obligations seriously?"

"With all due respect, your Honor, how do you expect me to pay my ex-wives if I'm not working? I need to work," Don said. "You have my word; I will take the alimony seriously."

Judge Syverson took another minute to review several more documents. When she was done, she stacked and straightened the papers and placed them back in the file.

"I have reached a decision," the judge said sternly. "The court is not satisfied with the financial information provided by Don Koch regarding his inability to pay alimony to Tiffany Koch and Lisa Bennett. The respondent is hereby remanded to the Hennepin County Jail until spousal maintenance is current."

Elizabeth stood quickly in her form-fitting white suit. "Your Honor, to Mr. Koch's point, and as you are aware, it is extremely difficult for someone who is incarcerated to earn a living," she said. "We ask that the court grant Mr. Koch work release privileges."

Judge Syverson considered the request for a brief moment. "Given the circumstances, Counselor, I'm not comfortable with such an arrangement."

Elizabeth nodded and sat down.

"This court is adjourned," the judge announced.

The strike of her gavel echoed through the courtroom. As she vacated the bench and returned to her chambers, deputies approached Don, instructed him to stand and cuffed his hands behind his back.

"You said I wouldn't get jail time!" Don barked at Elizabeth. "Do you even know what you're doing?"

"We'll get this straightened out," Bernard interjected.

"You better get it straightened out," Don seethed, his chin jutted toward Elizabeth. "Or get rid of her."

As the crowd made their way toward the exit, Maddie and Simone walked briskly toward Lisa Bennett. They met at the end of the first row of chairs.

"Hello, Ms. Bennett, my name is Madelyn Cummins." Maddie handed her a business card. "I'm a divorce attorney, and my firm is representing Jayne Koch. This is my paralegal, Simone Backstrom. May we have a minute of your time?"

Lisa's eyes lingered on Maddie's bruised face. "What's this regarding?" she asked.

"It appears you and Jayne Koch may have more in common than you know," Maddie said.

"How's that?" Lisa asked.

"During the discovery process, we learned about the trust your family set up for you," Maddie said. "Would you be willing to come to our office and discuss your ex-husband's involvement in it?"

Lisa looked from Maddie to Simone and to the front of the courtroom at the Minnesota state seal that adorned the wall beyond the judge's bench. She centered the diamond pendant on the gold chain she wore around her neck.

"Yes," she said finally.

"You asked to see a less expensive lot. This one is cheaper than those across the street, the main difference being the trees. If you were to build here, you wouldn't have the mature trees, but there will be new landscaping to buffer you from future neighbors. You would save $15,000," said Louis Olsen, a trim man in his early 60s. The warm breeze slightly mussed his white-blond hair as he pointed a finger in the direction of the undeveloped field.

"Show me where the property ends," the client said. "To give me a better feel for the lot's size."

"Sure," Louis said. "Watch your step."

The two men headed east across the field.

"My biggest concern is what my wife might think about the noise and dust from future construction," the client said.

"Royal Oaks is a more mature development," Louis said. "There are trade-offs in both areas. Here in Shady Grove the club house and pool won't be built for another year—"

"Whoa!" the client yelped as he stumbled and thrashed forward.

Louis took hold of his elbow to keep him upright. "Are you OK?" he asked. "This section is rockier than the others."

"I'm fine," the client replied.

Louis bent down to inspect an item that was not a rock. It was a large leather briefcase camouflaged with rusty-colored dust. Louis grabbed the case by its wide strap and steadied himself, taken aback by its weight.

"My father was an attorney," the client said. "He had a case like that for files."

"It's dirty, but it doesn't look like it's been here long," Louis said. "Maybe there's an ID."

He unzipped the briefcase. Tucked inside were manila folders organized by date, yellow legal pads with notes, and several loose documents. There was an identification tag that said: "Property of Madelyn Cummins, Esq. If lost, please return to Cummins Law Office, Stillwater, Minnesota."

"You're right, it belongs to an attorney," Louis said. "She is probably frantic with worry. I wonder how it ended up here?"

* * *

Simone could not identify the middle-aged man waiting in the reception area, but she immediately recognized Maddie's briefcase. Louis Olsen had called earlier and offered to drop it off. His luxury home company, Olsen Homes, was well regarded in the area, and Simone was impressed by his willingness to deliver it in person.

"Hello, Mr. Olsen, I'm Simone Backstrom, we spoke on the phone," she said and shook his hand. "Thank you so much for coming to the office. I can't begin to tell you how relieved Ms. Cummins is about the recovery of her files."

"No trouble at all," Louis said and handed her the case. "I suspected the contents were important. I'm glad there was identifying information, and everything was intact."

"May I ask where you found it? It looks like it's endured some of the elements."

"Yes. I was showing a client a lot in one of our brand-new developments. He tripped over it."

"Where is the lot located?" she asked.

"Near the commercial corridor adjacent to I-94."

"Mr. Olsen," Simone said and paused. "Ms. Cummins suffered an episode of transient global amnesia. The police found her wandering in the street in her pajamas, but she doesn't recall where she was or what she was doing."

"Is she all right?" he asked, his tone concerned.

"She is OK," Simone said. "She sustained some minor injuries and she's a bit shaken up, which is understandable given the circumstances."

"Is there something I can do to help?" Louis asked.

"If you could show us the exact location where the case was found, I think it might help Ms. Cummins recall what happened."

"I'd be happy to."

* * *

Maddie stood alongside Simone and Louis surveying the landscape. The wind picked up and cotton ball clouds moved rapidly against the bright blue sky. A swath of hair blew across Maddie's face. She fished an elastic hair tie from her pocket and cinched it around a low ponytail.

"We found your briefcase just over there, Miss," Louis said. He pointed toward a mound of dirt with a patch of flattened grass.

"Please, call me Maddie," she said with a smile. She had not been called "miss" since college.

"Do you recall being here?" Simone asked, her tone gentle, motherly.

"I vaguely recall standing in a field," Maddie said. "I may have slid down a hill." The images that came to her were fleeting, like a film being played too fast.

"Take in the view, Maddie," Simone said. "The presence of your briefcase puts you here. Does it look familiar?"

"In my recurring nightmare, I am in an area like this, and there is someone behind me," Maddie said. "And a skull. In the nightmare, I always find a human skull."

"Why is someone following you? Do you have something they want?" Simone asked, hoping to spark a memory.

"I have no idea why. I don't know what any of it means." Maddie's voice cracked.

"Oh, honey." Simone pulled Maddie in for a hug. "Amnesia has got to be such a frightening thing."

"I just want to know what happened," Maddie said.

"Not knowing has probably affected you more than you realize," Simone said.

"I'm sorry about what you're going through," Louis said.

"Thank you," Maddie said. "You've been so kind."

"Let's take a look around," Simone suggested.

The earth crunched beneath their feet as the three of them walked the lot.

"Olsen Homes owns the property up to the lot line, which you can see by the survey pins," Louis explained. "Beyond that is some of the last remaining land in Woodbury. No developers have come forward with plans to build on it."

"Why not?" Maddie asked.

"Too expensive," Louis said.

"Is it possible that someone was chasing me off the land in the middle of the night? Or that human remains are buried out there?"

"Not many folks come here after dark," Louis said. "Occasionally teenagers come here to hang out and drink, smoke pot, minor stuff." As he spoke the words, he stepped on a beer can. "They always leave their garbage." He retrieved the discarded can. "As for the remains, I've been doing this for a long time, and I can tell you it's common to find animal bones on job sites."

"It's probably just a story I created in my mind," Maddie said.

"I have to get going, but you're welcome to look around a

bit more if you like," Louis said. He bid the women farewell, addressed Maddie as "miss" once more and wished her the best.

"Louis Olsen is proof chivalry is not dead," Maddie said. "I'll take being called miss over ma'am any day."

Simone laughed and nodded.

Maddie looked out over the terrain, switchgrass swaying in the wind, wild prairie roses dotting sloping hills in dusty pink. None of it was familiar. She scanned the city skyline in the distance, its buildings almost out of view. For a moment, she recalled seeing the lights of those buildings against the dark summer sky and feeling drawn toward them. As quickly as the memory came, it vanished.

"Is there something else you remember?" Simone asked.

"The city lights on the horizon," Maddie said.

"Anything else?"

"No," Maddie said, feeling defeated. "I'm exhausted. Let's go."

"Have you talked to your primary care physician about your TGA experience?" Simone asked as they walked back to the car.

"I've got an appointment scheduled with my doctor next week. I'm hoping she can recommend a therapist. Paula has been doing some research, and apparently it's not uncommon to dream about lost memories after a bout of TGA."

"I'm glad you're going to talk to your doctor," Simone said, squeezing Maddie's arm. "I think your nightmares are happening for a reason. Suppose you did see or find something? Something that wasn't meant to be witnessed or uncovered? It might sound outlandish, and I know it hasn't been easy, but I think your dreams are trying to tell you something of importance."

"Paula thinks so, too."

After exploring the grounds where the briefcase was found, Simone insisted they stop at the Woodbury Police Department so Maddie could update Lt. Niles. At the police station, Maddie asked to speak with the lieutenant.

"He's off today," the officer at the reception desk said. "His partner, Officer Wilcox, is here. Would you like to speak with her?"

"Yes, please. My name is Madelyn Cummins. She may not remember me. She and Lt. Niles helped me last Saturday."

The receptionist nodded and stepped away from the desk.

"Honey, she'll remember you," Simone said. "You had amnesia, for heaven's sake. That's not a common occurrence, even for the police."

"Ms. Cummins," Officer Wilcox said as she approached, "it's good to see you." Her eyes scanned the mottled contusions on Maddie's face and arms.

"Call me Maddie, please. Officer Wilcox, this is my associate, Simone Backstrom."

"My cousin worked with your firm. She said you were two

of the best attorneys around," Officer Wilcox said as she shook Maddie's hand and then Simone's.

"I'm not an attorney," Simone corrected. "I'm Ms. Cummins' paralegal."

"She's more than a paralegal. She graduated at the top of her class at Hamline University School of Law. The firm would not be what it is without her."

"Well, that's true," Simone said with a chuckle.

"Sounds like you've got a great partnership," the officer said. "From my experience, the right partner makes all the difference in the world."

"I agree," Simone said.

"Ms. Cummins, thank you for your kind letter," Officer Wilcox said. "How are you doing?"

"As well as could be expected," Maddie said. "I still don't remember much."

"We do have some information to share," Simone said.

"Yes," Maddie said. "We stopped by to let you and Lt. Niles know that my briefcase was found by a real estate developer, Louis Olsen, who was showing a client a lot. All my files were inside."

"That's great. Do you have the specific location?"

"We met Mr. Olsen there today," Simone said.

"It's a new housing development called Shady Grove. It's off Glenn Road," Maddie said.

"Not far from where we found you," Officer Wilcox said.

"I don't recall where you found me," Maddie said, "and I don't think I would recognize it if I did."

"We're grateful Mr. Olsen was willing to show us the location. I hoped seeing where her briefcase was found might give her memory a little push," Simone said.

"It was only vaguely familiar," Maddie said. "But I'm relieved to have the case back."

The officer nodded and smiled warmly. "Thank you for the update. I'll let the lieutenant know you stopped by," she said. "And Ms. Cummins, please keep us updated on how you're doing."

"Thank you for your time, Officer," Simone said and turned to face Maddie. "Let's get you back to Paula's."

* * *

Maddie buckled herself into the passenger seat of Simone's Volvo and thought about Officer Wilcox's comment regarding partnerships. Maddie had planned to expand her legal practice, and Simone would make a fantastic law partner. First Maddie would need to convince her to take the bar exam.

"Simone, may I ask why you never sat for the bar?" she said.

"Well," Simone said and adjusted her leopard print sunglasses. "I was older than your average law student when I attended Hamline. By the time I graduated with my JD, I had three young children at home. Then Edward was diagnosed with cancer and our world was turned upside down. I needed to work to support our family, so I took a job as a paralegal at a firm in

St. Paul. I enjoyed the work. It kept a roof over our heads and food on the table."

They stopped at a red light. Maddie glanced over at Simone and watched her expression shift. She appeared lost in the moment. Traffic began to move, and once again Simone concentrated on the road.

"Edward's cancer went into remission, and he went back to work full-time—we were so thankful. We started to have conversations again about me taking the bar exam. As you know, studying for it is a full-time job, so it required some planning. As soon as we thought we had all our ducks in a row, Edward's cancer came back."

"I'm so sorry, Simone," Maddie said.

"When he died, I put every iota of strength I had into raising our girls. You know the rest. They struggled at first. And then they thrived. They went on to graduate from college, find careers they love. They're healthy and happy and creating the lives they envisioned for themselves."

Maya, Simone's oldest, was vice president of the IT division of a Fortune 500 company headquartered in the Twin Cities. Her middle child, Sasha, graduated from the University of Minnesota Medical School and partnered with another physician to open a women's clinic. Simone's youngest daughter, Arianna, majored in theater. She worked as a television actor in L.A. and had recently been accepted into the graduate program at Julliard.

"Your daughters could not have done it without your support," Maddie said. "And I would not be where I am today without you."

When Maddie decided to launch her firm as a newly minted attorney, she knew she'd need an experienced paralegal by her side. Simone had been a godsend. She was outspoken from the start, willing to share her opinion and give advice—often with a dose of tough love. As an only child who had lost both her parents before she graduated from law school, Maddie had gained an unexpected mother figure in Simone. Her daughters had become like Maddie's sisters.

"Family is a priority," Simone said. "I consider you part of ours."

"Simone, you have helped each of us to achieve our dreams," Maddie said. "When are you going to pursue yours? When are you going to become the attorney you were meant to be?"

"Oh, I don't know," Simone said. She waved the question away with her hand and shook her head of thick, shiny silver hair. "I'm content doing what I'm doing."

"I think it's time to focus on you. I know your girls would agree."

"Where is all this coming from, Maddie? I'm nearing 60. Most law offices aren't looking to hire an attorney my age."

"The firm is busier than we've ever been. I am ready to bring on another attorney. I would be thrilled if that partner was you."

"That's a lovely thought but—"

"It's never too late to pursue a dream, Simone! One of my law classmates was 60 when he graduated, and he is still practicing."

"I would have to pass the bar first," Simone said.

"The bar exam is the last week of February. That gives you six months to prepare. Please, Simone. Give it some thought."

"Did I mention I'm meeting with Lisa Bennett today?" Maddie asked as she poured a fruit smoothie from the blender into a glass. She took a seat at one end of Paula's kitchen island.

Paula was seated at the other end, tucking into a bowl of cereal. She held her up index finger as she finished chewing. "Mm-hmm," she nodded. "Has she agreed to let you review her trust documents?"

"She's bringing them with her," Maddie said.

"And you're meeting with Jayne this afternoon?"

"Yes," Maddie said, sipping her smoothie.

"Are you sure you're feeling up to a full day of work?"

"I think so," Maddie said. "Are you finished with the newspaper?"

"It's all yours," Paula said, handing that morning's Star Tribune to her friend. "Promise me you won't push yourself too hard today."

"Yes Mom, I promise," Maddie teased as she thumbed through the thin sheets of newsprint in search of the Metro section.

"I'm serious, Maddie," Paula said. "Rest is important to your recovery."

Maddie did not reply. Her eyes were fixed on a headline.

"What's wrong?" Paula asked, noting the sudden change in Maddie's demeanor.

"Listen to this: 'Children discover human remains in Shady Grove development.'"

"Keep reading," Paula said, eyes wide.

"Three boys playing in a vacant lot in the new Shady Grove development near Glenn Road in Woodbury found what is believed to be a human skull. Upon their discovery, the boys, twin brothers, age 10, and a friend, age 11, returned to the home of the twins and told their mother. She went back to the discovery site with the boys and called 911.

"Woodbury police cordoned off the area for excavation. A spokeswoman said little is known about the identity of the remains. 'The human skull has been taken into evidence, while investigators continue to search for additional remains. Forensic tests may take several weeks for a conclusive identification. Detectives are in the process of reviewing missing persons reports from the past several years. At this time, we are not certain if we are dealing with a homicide.'"

Maddie looked at Paula, her face devoid of color. She struggled to process what she'd read.

"You need to contact the police," Paula said.

"And say what? I've had visions about this skull? I have no idea what I saw, what really happened."

"Those bones were discovered in the Shady Grove

development, the place where Louis Olsen found your briefcase. You were there. What you think you saw was real. You are calling Lt. Niles this very minute."

* * *

Lt. Niles met Maddie and Paula just outside a large area that was cordoned off with yellow plastic crime tape. It was about a half block from where Maddie and Simone had been the day before. Maddie's chest tightened at the sight of technicians digging up human remains. She could barely breathe.

"Everything OK?" Lt. Niles asked.

"It's a bit surreal," Maddie said.

"If you need to take a break at any time, just say so," the lieutenant said.

Maddie nodded.

"The medical examiner inspected the skull and determined it is that of an adult male. The cause of death has not been determined. The bones have been here a while, perhaps as long as a decade. Far enough back to when this land was still being farmed."

Maddie was silent as she processed what the lieutenant was saying.

"What happens while the forensics team works on identifying the remains?" Paula asked.

"We start reviewing missing persons files to see if we can connect the bones to someone," Lt. Niles said. "We're in contact with state and federal law enforcement agencies as well."

"You'll approach it as a cold case?" Paula asked.

"If we can establish a positive ID, yes. We'll notify next of kin and open an investigation to try to find a potential motive or suspect."

"Is there anything I can do to help?" Maddie asked.

Lt. Niles turned toward Maddie and hooked his thumbs in his belt. "If you remember anything else about what happened the morning we found you—anything at all—please call me."

S till reeling from the morning's developments, Maddie checked her makeup in the restroom mirror. Finally, she had confirmation she'd actually found a human skull. The knowledge that it hadn't been the product of her imagination didn't make her feel better. It only raised more questions. For now, she had to push them out of her mind. Don Koch's first wife, Lisa, was soon to arrive, and Maddie needed to focus. She smoothed her hair and dabbed concealer on the faded bruises. She'd become accustomed to covering the splotches, now shades of yellowish green.

Maddie greeted Lisa in the lobby and escorted her to the conference room. Lisa sat, smoothed her cobalt blue tailored dress, and poured herself a cup of coffee from the carafe on the table.

"Thank you for coming," Maddie said.

"I almost changed my mind," Lisa said.

"May I ask why?"

"Don and I have been divorced for almost 20 years. I prefer to keep the past in the past where it belongs."

"I understand," Maddie said. "I appreciate your willingness

to discuss your ex-husband." Lisa nodded and took a sip of coffee. "Before we get started, Ms. Bennett, are you willing to testify in a court of law?" Maddie asked.

"Yes, I am," she said.

"Prior to the alimony hearing, had the two of you been in communication?"

"Not about the alimony," Lisa said.

"You've had contact otherwise?" Maddie asked.

"You might think, having had two children together, we would have had a need to communicate over the years. Don didn't play an active role as a parent, and our interactions had always been minimal. That changed about a year ago."

"What happened a year ago?"

"An envelope addressed to Don was delivered to my home. I thought it was junk mail, so I opened it. It was a check for $25,000."

"Was the check payable to Don?"

"No, it was made out to someone else."

"Do you recall the name?"

"No, I didn't know the name," Lisa said. "It was from PD Holdings."

"Are you familiar with PD Holdings?"

"Never heard of it," Lisa said.

"Do you recall the bank? Maddie asked.

"I believe it was Commonwealth Banc."

"Did Don offer an explanation?" Maddie asked.

"No." Lisa said. "He said he'd send a courier to pick it up. He asked about our daughters, Hazel and Anna. Got nostalgic about a trip we'd taken to Wisconsin Dells when the girls were little and the great time we had. He said he wanted to repair his relationship with them and claimed he reached out several times. He asked if I would be willing to facilitate a conversation."

"What was your response?" Maddie asked.

"I told him they were adults and made their own decisions. I reminded him that there were reasons they didn't communicate with him."

"Like what?" Maddie asked.

"Don has always had anger issues. When they were little, he would fly off the handle—yell and slam doors—if the girls interrupted him during a phone call or if they went into his home office. They were afraid of him. Later, when it came to determining custody and visitation, they wanted nothing to do with him. When I reminded him of this, he said I turned his kids against him and hung up on me. I asked the girls later if they'd heard from their dad recently, and they said they hadn't," Lisa said. "Not ever."

"Have you received mail for Don since then?"

Lisa nodded. "I leave it on the porch and text him and he sends a courier to pick it up."

"Have you considered marking the envelopes 'return to sender'?" Maddie asked.

"I've asked Don to notify the sender or have his mail forwarded," Lisa said. "He claims he has, and the issue is with the postal service."

"Are you comfortable sharing details about Don and your trust fund?"

Lisa scooted forward in her chair. She reached into her tote bag, pulled out a thick sheaf of papers and placed it on the table between them. Her trust, Lisa explained, was created by her parents when she was a child. Her three brothers also had them; they were revocable trusts meant to provide them with funds for education, to buy a home, potentially support them in old age.

Lisa unclipped the papers and handed specific pages to Maddie across the table. "After our daughters were born, Don suggested we make it a joint trust in both our names. He said it was in the girls' best interest. I asked how it was better for them; they were already the beneficiaries. He'd drop it for a while and then bring it up again."

Maddie looked over the original agreement and the amendment, which noted the trust of nearly $3 million had changed to joint ownership. She studied Don's signature—large and flamboyant.

"You eventually agreed," Maddie noted. "What made you change your mind?"

"In the early '90s, there was what he claimed was a once-in-a-lifetime opportunity to build a new golf course with a resort in Duluth, near Lake Superior. He negotiated land deals and met with a general contractor who had managed projects of the same scope. He said multiple funders were lined up; our investment would give us ownership rights. He had blueprints for the resort and an artist's rendering of the golf course. What he showed me was spectacular, and yet—" Lisa paused.

"And yet?" Maddie asked.

"I thought it might be out of his league. It's one thing to

sell cars and accumulate auto dealerships, but Don didn't know the first thing about real estate development or the hospitality industry. We discussed it, and he assured me he would hire the most knowledgeable people in the region. I talked with my mother about it, and based on the details Don provided, she thought it was a shrewd investment. Don was added to the trust and had access to those funds."

"What happened after that?"

"A year passed and progress on the development was minimal. Aside from the funders Don mentioned in our early conversations, no other investors were involved. I began to question everything."

Maddie reviewed a spreadsheet, running her finger down a column of numbers that gradually diminished in size. In less than two years, more than $2 million had been drawn from the trust fund. "You discussed your concerns with Don?" she asked.

"Yes," Lisa said. "He would rattle on about the scope of the project and everyone involved—the land planner, architects, engineers, the general contractor. He chartered a private plane and flew up to Duluth for meetings several times a month. He promised to take the girls and I with him numerous times."

"Did you ever join him?" Maddie asked.

Lisa shook her head. "Around Thanksgiving, a subcontractor whose crew had worked on the project called our home phone. I suggested he call Don at the office. He said his company had been waiting several months to be paid for work that had been completed. He had initially worked with the general contractor who had gone MIA. He demanded Don pay him and threatened to sue for breach of contract. I asked the amount due to his company. I'll never forget that moment—I couldn't move—he said he was owed in excess of a half-million dollars."

"What did you do?" Maddie asked.

"I took his information and contacted my lawyer. I asked for an immediate accounting of the trust, which I knew would take time. In the meantime, my attorney began working with a private investigator who looked into the general contractor and his company. What they found was shocking."

"The general contractor, Philip Lane, had been killed in an automobile accident six months earlier. Don never mentioned Philip by name. He never told me the general contractor had died, that his company was defunct, or that the work had halted. He continued to claim he was flying to Duluth to check on the progress of the project. He went so far as to tell me I would be pleased with how things were coming along."

"You didn't confront him?" Maddie asked.

"Per my attorney's recommendation, I waited for the accounting of the trust and said nothing. When I learned the fund had dwindled to barely a million dollars, I berated myself for not trusting my instincts. I knew Don didn't have the expertise to succeed in real estate. Being an avid golfer doesn't make you qualified to develop a golf resort."

"What happened when you finally confronted him?"

"He went to Florida for a business meeting. As soon as he left, the girls and I moved out of our house in Minnetonka and into my mother's house in Chanhassen. While he was still in Florida, I called and told him our marriage was over. I said I knew the golf resort was a bust and that he had drained millions from the trust."

"Did he deny it?"

"He blamed Philip Lane," Lisa said. She paused as she took a drink of coffee, placed the mug on the table, and twisted the large sapphire on her right ring finger.

As she did, Maddie noticed Lisa's hands were trembling. "Ms. Bennett, are you OK?" she asked.

Lisa clasped her hands together. "The private investigator found that Philip showed up at Koch Automotive Group demanding payment from Don. A few days later, Philip's car plunged 60 feet off a cliff. Don's version of what happened was that Philip stole the money intended for the subcontractors and used it to support a cocaine habit that ended up killing him."

"Did the investigator suspect foul play?" Maddie asked.

"Here's his report," Lisa said, pushing it over to Maddie. "The coroner determined Philip died early in the morning. Philip's office manager confirmed he was on his way to the job site. The Duluth police initially thought he had fallen asleep at the wheel. During the investigation they discovered green scuff marks from another vehicle on the driver's side of his pickup truck and thought he may have been run off the road. The paint from the scuff marks was difficult to analyze due to the severity of the damage to the vehicle. The results were inconclusive."

"Ms. Bennett," Maddie said, straightening her back. "Do you think your ex-husband is capable of murder?"

"There are people working for Don who are more like henchmen than salesmen. He surrounds himself with questionable characters that I have never been comfortable around. Some of them—Trey Calvers for one—I wouldn't let near my daughters. Hazel would burst into tears at the sight of that man." At the thought of it, Lisa's eyes filled with tears. When she started to speak again, she lost her words.

"Do you need a break?" Maddie asked.

"If you'll excuse me," Lisa said and stood. "Where's the restroom?"

In the silence of the conference room, Maddie wondered if people ever really change. Based on what she learned about Don from Jayne's divorce case, and what Lisa was telling her now, he had a pattern of manipulation and deception to get what he wanted. He seemed to do so with little regard for the damage it caused to the people he claimed to care about and his relationships.

Lisa returned after a few minutes looking fresh and composed.

"Are you OK to continue?" Maddie asked.

"Yes, thank you." Lisa said and sat. "The circumstances surrounding Philip Lane's death and the possibility Don may have had something to do with it was alarming. At that point, all I could think about was dissolving the marriage. Don was removed from the trust with my mother's help. I didn't bother trying to recoup the money he'd taken from the trust. I just cut my losses."

"I'm sorry you and your daughters went through that," Maddie said.

"It was a long time ago," Lisa said. "I'm surprised talking about it today made me so emotional."

"You're human," Maddie said. "I appreciate your willingness to revisit the details."

"I hope the information is helpful."

The meeting wrapped up and the women meandered to the lobby. Lisa paused at the door. "May I ask a favor?"

"Certainly," Maddie said.

"My daughter Hazel is in her third year of law school and in the process of choosing her area of specialty," Lisa said. "Would you be willing to meet with her and offer some advice?"

"Of course. Have her give me a call."

* * *

"Only a small percentage of divorce cases in Minnesota go to trial," Maddie informed Jayne.

After spending the first half of the day with the Woodbury police and then Lisa Bennett, her muscles had grown heavy with exhaustion. Still, she managed to keep her face neutral.

"If Don insists on going to trial, it will require more time and money. I will continue working to negotiate a settlement. That's my priority."

"What would a trial entail?" Jayne asked, uncrossing and crossing her slender tan legs.

"There isn't a jury," Maddie said. "A judge in family court hears and decides on the matter."

"Like the judge who sent Don to jail?"

"Yes," Maddie said. "After the trial, attorneys for both parties have 30 days to submit a proposed order with the terms each would like to see in the divorce judgment. I would also submit a memorandum of the law to support the proposal. It could be as long as 90 days before the judge chooses one of the proposals or creates a new one that incorporates terms from both."

"God, I hate this," Jayne said. She took a sip of water. Her lipstick left a bright smear of pink on the glass. "Leaving this relationship is for the best, but Gabby doesn't deserve to be in the middle of it."

"Divorce can be especially difficult when young kids are involved," Maddie acknowledged. "You should also know, in Minnesota, divorce trials take place in open court. Anyone could walk into the courtroom—neighbors, coworkers, members of the media—and learn the most confidential details of your marriage and its breakdown."

"So my personal business could be out there for the world to read about and comment on?" Jayne asked.

"Yes, I'm sorry," Maddie said. "Let's not borrow trouble where there may be none. With the potential criminal charges Don is facing, his legal team should be advising him against a divorce trial. We'll know more after he is released from jail."

Jayne stared at the artwork that hung on the conference room wall. "I'm certain Don is not being forthcoming about assets," she said, her eyes fixed on the painting. "Has anything turned up in your investigation?"

"Are you familiar with a company called PD Holdings?" Maddie asked.

"I'm not," Jayne said. "Should I be?"

At the coffee shop down the block from the law office, Maddie sat at a table near the large front window. Sunlight streamed in, illuminating the fronds of the potted ferns hanging from the ceiling. She checked her makeup while she waited for her latte to cool. As she dabbed pressed powder from a compact onto the lingering bruise on her cheek, she was approached by a woman in her 20s in a casual black jersey knit dress, gold hoop earrings and fashionable tortoise shell glasses. Her light brown hair was piled into a messy bun. "Excuse me," the woman said. "Are you Madelyn Cummins?"

"Please, call me Maddie," she said, snapping the compact shut and tossing it in her bag. "You must be Hazel Koch."

"Hazel Bennett," she corrected, offering her hand to Maddie. "I legally changed my name about a year ago."

"It's nice to meet you, Hazel," Maddie said, standing partially to shake it.

"I appreciate you taking time out of your schedule to talk with me." Hazel crinkled her nose. "I know my mother asked you to do this, but is it weird? Since you're the attorney for my bio father's third wife?"

"A little unusual," Maddie admitted, noting Hazel's use of the term "bio father" the way people who'd been adopted often did. "But we're not here to talk about that. I'm always happy to meet with other women interested in legal careers."

As Hazel smiled in relief, a deep dimple appeared on her right cheek. "I'm going to grab a coffee; do you need anything?"

"No thanks, I'm all set," Maddie said, raising her latte as if she were making a toast.

When Hazel returned, she sat across from Maddie and adjusted her glasses, obviously examining the splotches on Maddie's face. "I'm sorry if this is too personal," she said, ripping open and emptying the contents of two sugar packets into her coffee. "May I ask what happened to you?"

"It's not too personal," Maddie said with a small smile. "I experienced an episode of transient global amnesia."

"That sounds serious," Hazel said.

Maddie hesitated for a second. "The police found me wandering in the street in my pajamas just before sunrise," she said. "I'd been out there for hours. I have no memory of it."

"Were you sleepwalking?" Hazel asked, eyes fixed on Maddie's.

"No," Maddie said. "Apparently, I was awake and conscious before I experienced TGA, but where I was, what I was doing, how I got these scrapes and bruises during that time, it's all a mystery."

"So those memories are, like, repressed?" Hazel asked.

"More like erased," Maddie said. "I've had some vague

recollections of that night. According to the doctor who diagnosed me, I may never remember what happened before."

"I'm so sorry. That must be a weird feeling," Hazel said, her face showing sincere concern. "I hope I'm not overstepping, but I have an amazing therapist, Samantha Kopet, who helped me access repressed memories from my childhood. Even if your memories of that night are gone for good, it might be worth talking to someone like her. I think I have her card." She took the wallet out of her bag and thumbed through its contents. "Here it is."

"Thank you, Hazel, that's very kind," Maddie said. She tucked the card into the side pocket of her bag. "Now let's talk about you."

Hazel shared that she'd attended the University of Wisconsin-Madison for pre-law and was in her third year at Mitchell Hamline School of Law. She'd initially envisioned a role as in-house counsel for one of Minnesota's corporate giants—working for Target had been a longtime dream. Competition was said to be stiff for positions there, but she was at the top of her class, so it hadn't deterred her. After not being offered an internship at Target as she'd hoped, and accepting and completing an internship at Best Buy instead, Hazel had begun to have a change of heart. She couldn't see herself as a cog in giant corporate machine. It bothered her that corporations were often motivated by the bottom line instead of the well-being of their employees and the community.

"So you're thinking about family law?" Maddie asked.

"Yeah," Hazel said. "Is that crazy?"

"Not at all," Maddie said. "What draws you to it specifically?"

"I want to use my law degree for good. I studied collaborative family law as an elective last semester, and something just clicked. Finding solutions to family legal issues seems to come naturally to me."

"Family law attorneys play a vital role in helping people navigate some of the most poignant periods of their lives. You can do a lot of good with a family law focus."

"Yes, but what are the not-so-great parts of the job?" Hazel asked. "Without the sugarcoating."

"Well, you'll probably make less money than you would in corporate law," Maddie said bluntly.

"That's OK," Hazel said. "I read somewhere that the happiest lawyers are the ones who are the lowest paid."

"I'm not so sure about that," Maddie said with a laugh.

"What else?" Hazel asked.

"Your schedule will not be dictated by you. You'll be subject to the demands of clients, the court, the partners you work for. I started a solo practice because I wanted autonomy and a bit more control over my time. That hasn't exactly gone as planned. I spend way more time working than I thought I would."

"Do you love the work?"

"I do," Maddie acknowledged. "It can be heartbreaking, especially when a child's welfare or justice for an abused spouse is at stake. It can be frustrating dealing with delays or the fact that sometimes no one really wins. I can confidently say that in nearly every case I've been involved with, my legal expertise has helped that individual or family and made their lives better in some way."

Maddie went on to describe her typical workday. One of the aspects she appreciated about her work was that it was never predictable or boring. They discussed the type of day-to-day tasks Hazel found fulfilling. Hazel shared details about her personal strengths and how she thought they might be helpful in the role.

"Aside from a solid understanding of the law, what skills do you think are most important to the success of a family law attorney?" Hazel asked.

"Clients are often very emotional, and understandably so," Maddie said. "You must be able to put yourself in their shoes, to imagine what it might be like for them, and to treat them with compassion and kindness throughout the process. You also need to be able to take emotion out of it so you can apply logic and solve the problem. It's a fine line. I think a great family lawyer is someone who can be empathetic and understanding without becoming too emotionally involved in their client's life."

Maddie looked at her watch; she was surprised 45 minutes had already passed. "It's been lovely chatting with you, Hazel," she said. "I have to get going."

"Thank you so much for taking time to meet with an up-and-coming attorney like me," Hazel said.

"Just curious," Maddie said, swirling the liquid in the bottom of her cup. "What made you want to study law in the first place?"

"Honestly?" Hazel said and paused.

Maddie didn't press for details. She had mastered the art of the silent pause as a tool for getting others to say more. She took the final gulp of her cold latte.

"Don Koch," Hazel said. "Spending my formative years around a man with no morals influenced who I wanted to be when I grew up. Which is the exact opposite of him."

Maddie pulled up a chair to Simone's desk. The webpage for PD Holdings, the name of the company that had mailed checks to Don at his first wife's address, was displayed on the screen. No individual or corporation was listed as the owner of the business. Simone entered the address listed on the website into the search bar. Google Maps produced an image of a parking lot.

A second search of the business name produced a different address in Edina—it appeared to be a parking lot as well. Simone clicked the street view and rotated the image slightly. Two single-story structures came into view. One had a loading dock with four bays. Beyond the buildings were two red metal sculptures that resembled large sails.

"I know where this is," Maddie said. "It's more of an industrial area. There's a strip mall across the street."

Simone clicked the mouse to rotate the image and zoom in. At one end of the strip, there were several businesses and a nearly full parking lot. "Looks like a dental office, an insurance agency—" she observed.

The other end of the strip appeared vacant, and there weren't any vehicles parked nearby.

"Let's go see it for ourselves," Maddie said.

* * *

Simone pulled into the strip mall's lot and parked. Canvas awnings capped each of the businesses' entrances. The women got out of the car and strolled the length of the strip, glancing inside the suites. There was a pet groomer in one suite, a State Farm office in another, a bustling dental clinic in the next one. And several others after that. They all appeared to be professional, well-maintained businesses.

On the opposite end, at the second to last suite, on the glass door, "IRS Tax Relief Services" was stenciled in small white letters. Inside, the building was dark.

"This must be seasonal," Maddie said. She pulled at the handle of the door; it was locked.

Simone took out her phone and searched for the business. "They've got a website. It's pretty generic. No photos of the staff, just a logo, an 800 number and a contact form."

"I see a reception desk and a waiting area. A couple of doors leading to what appear to be offices," Maddie said, peering inside.

The two of them walked toward the last suite where the strip ended. A sign that said "PD Holdings" was taped to the door, which was also locked. There were no lights on, and no one was inside. Against the wall, there was a cheap laminate desk, an outdated PC and a black office chair. Next to the desk, there was a printer on a stand. The floor was bare cement, no carpeting or tile. Simone pressed her phone to the window and took photos.

"I'll be right back," Maddie said when she spotted a full-figured woman standing at a row of gray metal mailboxes nearby. "Excuse me—"

The woman turned toward Maddie, her face thick with makeup. Her arms were full of magazines, large envelopes, letters and promotional mailers.

"Hi there," the woman said cheerfully.

"Hello," Maddie said and returned the smile. "Do you happen to know what kind of business PD Holdings is?"

"I'm sorry, I don't. None of the other business owners here seem to know much about them or the tax service."

"Let me help you," Maddie said and grabbed the stack of magazines.

"Oh, thank you," the woman said, shifting her arms. "Personally, I don't think they're legitimate," she whispered conspiratorially.

"What makes you say that?" Maddie asked.

"The tax place is only open half the year, and the other office is almost always empty. I've seen an older gentleman there a few times, but only when I'm here late or working on a Saturday. Everyone else I've seen there looks a bit suspicious."

"Suspicious?" Maddie asked.

"Muscle-bound, lots of tattoos, looking cocksure, like they're ready for a fight."

"May I ask where you work?" Maddie said.

"I'm a State Farm agent. I'm here every other Saturday." She walked at a leisurely pace toward her suite.

"That's when you've seen the older man?" Maddie asked.

"Yes, you can't miss him. He's got an expensive red sports car. Speeds through the lot. Parks diagonally across two spaces."

"Do you remember the make or model of the car?"

"A Mercedes hardtop convertible."

"Can you describe the man?" Maddie asked.

"Older. I'd say 60s. White hair. He's fit for his age." She stopped at the entrance of the State Farm office. "Are you a cop?" the woman asked.

"Forgive me, I haven't introduced myself. My name is Maddie Cummins. I'm an attorney."

"C'mon in. I'll give you my info."

The woman led Maddie into the well-appointed office. Maddie set down the stack of magazines while the woman removed a business card from a shiny metallic card holder on the reception desk.

"Sue Primrose."

"Thank you, Ms. Primrose. Do you know how long the white-haired man has been utilizing the space?"

"A year and a half, maybe two. The tax service has been here for years, but like I said, they only use the office six months out of the year."

"Have you ever received mail or deliveries for PD Holdings by mistake?"

"I haven't," Sue said. "I think some of the other businesses have."

"OK. Thank you for your time, Ms. Primrose," Maddie said.

"Sure thing," Sue said. "Let me know if there's anything else I can help you with."

* * *

"IRS Tax Relief Services has a litany of complaints against them," Maddie said, scrolling through her phone as Simone drove back to the office. "Based on dozens of angry customer reviews on Yelp!, it seems they're in the business of exploiting immigrants with tax problems."

"Sounds like someone needs to alert the attorney general's office," Simone said.

"Sue Primrose, the State Farm agent I spoke with, seemed to know more about PD Holdings than the tax business," Maddie said. "An older man, tall with white hair, shows up in the evening and on weekends. He drives a red Mercedes convertible."

"The staff at Best Smiles gave a similar description. Apparently, Mr. Mercedes showed up there to collect a package that was too large to fit in the mailbox. The receptionist light-heartedly said she thought he'd forgotten about it, and he berated her, brought her to tears. The dentist, Dr. Best, overheard the exchange and stepped out of the exam room to intervene. Mr. Mercedes rattled off a bunch of expletives and left in a huff. Sounds a lot like Don Koch."

"Yes, it does," Maddie agreed.

"PD Holdings could be a front company he's using to hide assets," Simone said.

"Sue mentioned that there'd been other suspicious men there, too," Maddie said. "I wonder if there are security cameras in the complex."

"If not, there are probably cameras on the warehouse properties across the street," Simone said. "I'll see what I can find."

"I'll connect with Sue again to find out who the landlord is," Maddie said.

"Great idea," Simone said.

"I'll also ask her to contact me when Mr. Mercedes returns. If we can get a license plate number, we can find out who it's registered to."

S imone discovered that a company called Commercial Pros
  owned and managed the complex where PD Holdings was
located. "Commercial Pros has exactly one employee who is
also the sole proprietor—a man named William Parker," she
said, handing Maddie a sheet of paper from the printer.

Maddie reviewed the image of a strikingly handsome man
with jet black hair and piercing blue eyes. He looked to be in his
late 50s or early 60s.

"Here's an aerial view of the address I found for Commercial
Pros," Simone said, handing Maddie a second sheet of paper
with the image of undeveloped empty field along the interstate.
"There's nothing there."

"Interesting," Maddie said.

"Commercial Pros has an EIN, but it isn't licensed with the
secretary of state's office, not even as a DBA. Mr. Parker also
owns several residential properties in Wayzata. Those appear to
be managed by a different enterprise than the business complex
in Edina. He was previously employed by Sven Johnson
Custom Homes."

Maddie was familiar with the once-prominent home builder. "How long did he work for Sven Johnson?"

"Twenty-five years. He left in 2008 before the market crashed and the company folded."

"Have you found anything that connects William Parker and Don Koch? Something that explains Don's connection to PD Holdings?" Maddie asked.

"Nothing yet," Simone said.

"I'm meeting with Sue Primose this evening," Maddie said. "Perhaps she'll have some information about her landlord that will be useful."

* * *

Maddie and Sue met for drinks at a crowded Edina restaurant not far from Sue's office. They ordered beverages and an appetizer to share and made small talk until the food arrived.

"How long has William Parker been your landlord?" Maddie asked as the server placed a plate of fried calamari on the table.

"Five or six years." Sue squeezed lemon on the calamari, forked several rings and piled them on her plate. "When I opened my office 10 years ago, the building was owned by an out-of-state property management company. It was sold a couple of years later to Commercial Pros. I assumed it was a large company with a full-time staff and maintenance team."

"It's not?" Maddie asked as she sipped her wine.

"No, it's a one-man operation," Sue said as she stirred her whiskey sour with the swizzle stick and took a drink. "At first, when Commercial Pros took over, whenever anything needed to be repaired, William Parker was impossible to reach. I dealt with a leaking toilet for months that he refused to fix or replace. Other tenants had similar issues. We compiled our list of grievances and threatened to report him to the state."

"You could have taken him to court," Maddie said.

"We would have, but he did a 180. Just the threat of a lawsuit was enough. After that, whenever something needed to be repaired, he was on it. That's not to say he's a great landlord—he's not. He does just enough to fly under the radar. There's been a lot of turnover with tenants. As I mentioned, there are some tenants with questionable businesses."

"What about security? Is Commercial Pros responsible for keeping the property secure per the terms of your lease?" Maddie asked.

"Yes, and there are security cameras, but who knows if they're operational," Sue said.

"What makes you say that?"

"With the previous owner, all of the businesses were connected to a live stream of video from cameras in and around our suites. We could all keep an eye on things, plus a security team monitored the complex and was available 24 hours a day. Now live video is streamed from the cameras on the property and fed to one central location. A security company that we know nothing about monitors them. If they aren't being monitored, or if the cameras aren't functioning, we have no way of knowing."

Sue shared stories about skateboarders using the strip to practice flips and tricks, a homeless man breaking into cars in the parking lot in search of valuables, teenagers spray painting obscenities on the back of the building, and other minor incidents. "It seems to me," she said, shaking the ice in her low ball glass, "these kinds of things don't happen when a property is secure."

"Why do you stay? Are you all locked into a long-term lease?" Maddie asked.

"I have five years left on my lease. I paid big bucks to remodel my suite a few years ago when I expanded my team. The location is ideal for me, my employees, my clients. These things aren't easy to come by."

"As a fellow business owner, I completely understand," Maddie said.

"Where is your office?" Sue asked.

"In Stillwater," Maddie said and reached in her purse for a business card. "We're in a charming historical building there. I'm ready to expand as well."

Sue wiped her hands on her napkin, took the card and examined it. "Family law," she said, noting Maddie's specialty. "Is the creep from PD Holdings involved in a case you're working on?"

"Possibly," Maddie said. "My expertise is in family law, but I'm happy to answer any legal questions you might have. Reach out anytime."

"I appreciate it, hon," Sue said and took the last swallow of her drink.

"May I ask one more favor?" Maddie said.

"Of course."

"When the red Mercedes shows up again, will you let me know? Text me the license plate number if you can?"

"You bet I will," Sue said.

"Freedom Financial filed a lawsuit in federal bankruptcy court this morning," Simone updated Maddie as they ate lunch at the office. She blew on a spoonful of steaming vegetable soup. "It states $635 million of Don Koch's debt is not dischargeable."

"Can you even fathom being $635 million in debt?" Maddie asked, eating a forkful of salad.

"How about $842 million? That's the sum of what Don owes all of his creditors," Simone said.

"Mind-boggling."

"Equally as astounding is how he claims to be broke but flaunts his wealth like he's on an episode of 'Lifestyles of the Rich and Famous.'" Simone shook her head in disbelief. "That reminds me, tomorrow's the day he is being released from county jail. Rumor has it Justice Syverson is going to demand the names of the individuals or organizations that have been funneling cash to him and bailing him out. We should be there."

"I agree," Maddie said, stabbing a pepper on her plate. "I shared the information about PD Holdings with Paula. She wasn't familiar with the company. She planned to share it with

Constance and the criminal investigation team. She said it's likely Don will be indicted on criminal charges within the next two weeks."

* * *

In family court, Maddie and Simone sat in the row of chairs behind the divorce attorneys for Don Koch's ex-wives; Tiffany Koch and Lisa Bennett were not present. There was an obvious change in Don's appearance. He looked disheveled and grimy—as if he hadn't showered in days—in his faded county jail jumpsuit.

"Mr. Koch, I sentenced you to jail for failure to pay alimony to both your first and second wives," Justice Syverson said. "You are being released because you have fulfilled the first condition, which was paying $5,000 in outstanding alimony to Tiffany Koch and another $3,000 to Lisa Bennett."

"Thank you, your Honor," Don said.

"I expect you to take the other conditions of your release seriously, which includes providing information about your income and expenses."

"I understand, your Honor," Don said.

"Mr. Koch, I would like to know about the $5,000 cash you were carrying at the time you were booked into jail last week. What can you tell me about it?"

"Your Honor, I—" Don stammered, glancing quickly at his attorney, Elizabeth, who was seated next to him in a rose-hued suit. "I wasn't expecting to be taken to jail last week. It's for household expenses. I didn't realize I needed to mention it."

"Where did the money come from, Mr. Koch?" the judge asked, her expression stoic.

"Your Honor—" Don began and paused as Elizabeth whispered in his ear.

"Mr. Koch, as you now know, incarceration is not a pleasant experience," the judge said, growing impatient. "Unless you want to go through that experience again, you must be transparent and truthful about your financial situation."

"Your Honor, if I may?" Don's divorce attorney Elizabeth interjected. "We intend to satisfy the conditions of this court. However, some of the financial information this court has requested could have bearing on Mr. Koch's criminal case."

Judge Syverson glared at Elizabeth. "Counselor, if you are intimating that Mr. Koch intends to plead the fifth, let me remind you that this right does not allow for someone to withhold information."

"We are aware of that your Honor. We have not intentionally withheld information, nor would we do so."

"Mr. Koch, I will ask you again, where did the $5,000 cash come from?"

"It was given to me by a friend, your Honor," Don said, his forehead glossy.

"What is the name of this generous friend who supplied you with cash?"

Don hesitated. "Victor Price," he said finally.

Maddie made note of the name in her phone.

"Thank you, Mr. Koch," Justice Syverson said. "I expect

you to submit an accounting to the court every week regarding money you are receiving or benefiting from. If you do not provide this information, or if you do not continue to meet your alimony obligations, I will revoke your release and send you back to jail. Do you understand?"

"Yes, your Honor," Don said.

"Mr. Koch, I hope you resolve to get your affairs in order. I don't wish to see you in my courtroom again," the judge said. "This court is adjourned."

Maddie's state of consciousness floated between almost asleep and nearly awake. Early birds chirped loudly, competing with the thoughts in her head for attention. Resigned to the fact that deep sleep was not in her immediate future, she peeled back the blanket. She slid her feet into her slippers, made the bed and went upstairs.

She opened her laptop at the dining room table, logged in to the background check website and searched for Victor Price in Minnesota. The first person in the list of results was a partner at Baylor and Price, a Twin Cities-based accounting firm. She downloaded the report and checked the business website. On the contact page, there was a photo of Victor Price. He was in his 60s with dark eyes and bushy dark eyebrows. He was completely bald; not a hint of stubble graced his bulbous head.

Maddie searched social media and found Baylor and Price's Facebook page, which was inactive, and Victor's personal page. He had thousands of friends and posted on the platform often. Pictures of exotic vacations were plentiful. Several were taken on boats in tropical locations like Tahiti, Bali and Hawaii. In many of the photos Victor's scalp was leathery red and sunburned, despite his olive complexion. He often wore a loud Hawaiian print shirt. There was almost always a cocktail in one hand, and sometimes a cigar in the other hand or clenched between his teeth.

Maddie skimmed Victor's information. His relationship status was listed as divorced. She easily found his ex-wife, Laura Price, who was pictured in many of the older posts on Victor's page. She appeared much younger than Victor.

Paula's soft footsteps approached the dining room from the hallway. "Up at the crack of dawn again I see."

"Can't sleep," Maddie said. "I'm searching for information about a man named Victor Price. Don mentioned him in family court yesterday afternoon."

"He did?" Paula said. She took a seat at the table.

"Yes. Do you know the name?"

"Yes," Paula said, shifting to the edge of her seat. "He's a person of interest in the criminal case. How did it come up in family court?"

"Don had five grand in his pocket the day Judge Syverson put him in jail. She wanted to know where it came from," Maddie said. "After stalling a bit, he said his friend Victor Price gave it to him."

"I can't believe he admitted that," Paula said. "We just confirmed Victor Price gave Don close to a half-million dollars, some of which he used to replenish his 401(k). Constance and her team planned to bring Victor in for questioning."

"So Jayne was right, Don is definitely hiding assets," Maddie said. She turned her attention back to the computer. "I noticed

Victor changed his relationship status to divorced on Facebook a couple of months ago. What are the odds he gifted Don the money, so he'd have fewer assets to divide in the dissolution of his own marriage?"

"I'd say the odds are good, but that's not my concern," Paula said. "If he knows Don outed him in court, there's a good chance Victor will make himself scarce to avoid questioning." She stepped into the bedroom to grab her phone from the nightstand. When she returned, she was scrolling through her contacts. "This could put a wrench in the criminal case."

"Are you calling Constance now?" Maddie asked. "It's barely 5 a.m."

"Knowing Constance, she's been up for a while," Paula said with a yawn.

"I'll make coffee," Maddie said.

* * *

"You are never going to believe this!" Simone shouted from the reception area.

Maddie had just finished a call with a client. She placed the receiver in the cradle and joined Simone at her desk. "What's up?" she said.

"You asked me to find out more about Victor Price," Simone said, pointing to a black and white image of two dozen young men in hockey gear lined up on the ice for a team photo. "There was a photo on Victor's Facebook that was taken at a recent class reunion for Cretin High School. When he attended in the

'70s, it was a private all-boys school—in the late '80s, it merged with its all-girls counterpart, Derham Hall, and became Cretin-Derham High School. I searched school records and found Don Koch was also a Cretin High graduate. Same year as Victor Price. They both played hockey."

"Wow," Maddie said. "Don and Victor's relationship goes back decades."

Maddie and Simone's conversation was interrupted by a text from Paula. "Press conference is about to start," the text said. "Turn on channel five."

As Simone turned on the television in the conference room, the bankruptcy trustee Colin Towles began to address a multitude of reporters from local and statewide news organizations. Paula stood next to him.

"Information about Don Koch's finances that have bearing on his bankruptcy have been made public," he said. "In a signed affidavit, Don Koch confirmed Victor Price gifted him in excess of $500,000. This money was used in part to replenish a 401(k) account, which Mr. Koch cashed out before filing bankruptcy, and to fund daily living expenses."

Reporters shouted questions that overlapped one another. Colin pointed to a tall brunette wielding a microphone.

"What is Don Koch's relationship with Victor Price?" the reporter asked.

"Victor Price is a partner at Baylor and Price, a CPA firm in Minneapolis that at one time handled all of the accounting for Koch Automotive Group."

CHAPTER TWENTY-ONE

"Who ordered the affidavit?" a rosy-cheeked blonde reporter asked.

"Justice Kathleen Syverson. In family court hearings regarding Don Koch's tardy alimony payments to his first and second wives, Justice Syverson asserted Mr. Koch has a legal obligation to reveal the identity of all financial donors."

"Were other donors named?" a wiry reporter in a sweat-stained shirt shouted.

Standing next to Colin, Paula looked out at the crowd of journalists hopping like cats on hot pavement, eager to file a story.

"No other donors were named in the affidavit. However, we have confirmed that Commonwealth Banc, owned by brothers Addison and Brandon McGuinn, aided Don Koch in hiding assets. Charges have been filed against all three men and their businesses."

Back in the conference room at Cummins Law Office, Maddie turned toward Simone. "Lisa Bennett mentioned Commonwealth Banc when we met," she said. "The check from PD Holdings that she opened by mistake—the one addressed to Don and made out to someone else—it was drawn from a Commonwealth Banc account."

At the press conference, as more questions erupted from the media, Colin raised his voice and continued: "U.S. Attorney Paula Milton will further address the charges filed against Commonwealth Banc."

Paula stepped forward and spoke. "Commonwealth Banc was holding several items of high value belonging to Mr. Koch, including Rolex watches and Cartier jewelry estimated to be worth over $1 million. Additionally, Commonwealth Banc made loans totaling $15 million to Don Koch without sufficient collateral. Neither the jewelry nor the loans were included in Mr. Koch's debt in his bankruptcy filing. We believe the McGuinn brothers and Don Koch colluded to hide Mr. Koch's assets and to keep Commonwealth Banc from being shut down by federal regulators."

"How did they do it?" a reporter shouted.

"Mr. Koch received funds from lenders like Freedom Financial to purchase inventory for American Car Rental, which was instead funneled directly to Commonwealth Banc—" Paula paused as Colin whispered in her ear.

"We have just learned the McGuinn brothers have filed suit in U.S. Bankruptcy Court to have the charges dismissed," Paula said.

Colin leaned toward the microphone as reporters continued to shout. "No further questions at this time," he said. "Thank you."

As the TV returned to regularly scheduled programming, Maddie eyes remained fixed on the screen. "Commonwealth Banc is well-regarded in this region. The McGuinn family has been one of the wealthiest families in Minnesota for generations. How did they get mixed up in this mess?"

It was finally moving day. Maddie stood at the intersection of the entryway, kitchen and living room of her new home, coordinating the movers.

"Unroll the rug in front of the fireplace, please," she said to one of them. "Those boxes all go in the kitchen," she directed two others.

As cardboard boxes were stacked three and four high next to the kitchen island, Maddie's phone buzzed with an incoming text from Sue Primrose: "The Mercedes was in the lot today," it said. It was immediately followed by a photo of a Minnesota license plate.

Maddie went into the screened porch off the dining area, away from the bustle of the movers. The day was cooler than average, around 80 degrees, a much-needed break from what had already been an oppressively hot summer. She sent Sue her thanks and scrolled through the contacts in her phone until she found the name she was looking for, Terri Cheloha, a friend from college who studied law enforcement and was now a member of the Minnesota State Patrol. She forwarded the license plate and asked Terri if she had time to pull the owner information. She knew it might be a day or two before she got a response; the summer months were busy for the State Patrol. Maddie was fine with that. The tasks before her were immense. She had dozens of boxes to sort through and hundreds of items to organize in cabinets, drawers and closets. She had to decide which items she'd display on the built-in bookshelves surrounding the fireplace.

The movers arranged the living room furniture on the rug per Maddie's instruction. She hoped it might give her a sense of accomplishment. It didn't. She felt like she'd been running in place all day.

As the parade of movers continued coming in and out of the house, Simone and Paula marched in with them. Paula held up two bags with salads from a nearby deli and announced, "Lunch is here!"

Simone carried a large vase filled with colorful blooms, which she placed on the island. "Oh, Maddie, your home is gorgeous," she said as she looked around.

"How can you tell?" Maddie asked with a sigh. "On the contrary, those flowers are undeniably beautiful. Thank you."

"You're welcome. You know, you don't have to unpack everything today," Simone said. "Give yourself time to decide where you want everything to go."

"Simone's right," Paula added. "You're staying at my place until your new bedroom furniture arrives next week. We have plenty of time to get you settled."

"I won't let you spend another minute of your precious time helping me get settled," Maddie said. "I can manage."

"Don't be silly," Paula said. "You would do the exact same thing for us."

"That's right," Simone said as she pulled Maddie in for a side hug. "You gave me plenty of your precious time when I moved into a house closer to the office,"

"Thank you," Maddie said, leaning into Simone. "I'm sure I'll need more reminders that this doesn't need to be done all at once."

* * *

The illuminated numbers on the nightstand clock read 4:17 a.m. As if it couldn't be right, Maddie tapped her phone, which displayed the exact same time. Her mind flashed to the morning Lt. Niles and Officer Wilcox had found her wandering in her pajamas. She recalled asking them what time it was and wondering how it could possibly be right.

Maddie sighed and rolled over, away from the window. The blinds were closed, but the light of dawn would seep through the slats soon. Her thoughts continued to spin. During her waking hours, her TGA experience existed in the murky past. The moment she started to drift off, the few pre-TGA memories she could recall played on repeat. Those memories refused to give her peace or a sound night's sleep.

Lately she'd been having a recurring nightmare about skeletal remains. A full skeleton, all 206 bones, like the ones she and Simone watched being unearthed and laid on a tarp at the site where the skull was found. The skeleton in her nightmare was not in pieces. It was intact and came for her with its bony fingers. And it had a voice. "Help me!" it demanded.

At 4:32 a.m., wide awake, Maddie got up, made the bed, grabbed her phone and padded up the steps. A sliver of moon still hung in the sky outside the kitchen window. She made coffee and checked her phone. There were several texts from friends congratulating her on the move. There was also a text with a link to a report from Terri, which she hadn't expected so soon.

"The vehicle is registered to Peter Allen Dickrell of Minneapolis. Hope this is helpful. Let's have lunch soon and catch up!"

Maddie clicked on the report. There was a driver's license photo of a handsome man sporting a thick thatch of white hair, just as Sue Primose had described. She sat at the dining room table, scrolled through the vehicle registration details, turned on her laptop and sipped her coffee.

Early in her legal career, before deciding to specialize in the collaborative and mediation family law process, Maddie tried her hand at personal injury. In the same way some attorneys swore off family law as a hotbed of drama, she found personal injury law to be exhausting, even if most cases settled before going to court. But she did enjoy the process of discovery and found it was almost never dull.

She entered Peter Dickrell's information into the background check website. As she stood to pour herself a second cup of coffee, Paula appeared in the kitchen in her pajamas.

"Good morning," her friend said, arms stretched overhead. "How long have you been up?"

"Not long," Maddie said.

"You're a terrible liar," Paula said.

"Sorry if I woke you," Maddie said, handing Paula a cup of coffee as a peace offering. "My time has been well spent. Terri sent me the information on Mr. Mercedes. His name is Peter Dickrell."

"That name sounds familiar," Paula said with a yawn.

Maddie began to scroll through the background report. Peter's parents were deceased. He had one surviving sibling who resided in Florida. He had been married at least twice.

Paula cradled her mug and read over Maddie's shoulder. "Scroll back up," she said, pointing at the screen. "There."

"Tiffany Joy Dickrell Koch," Maddie said.

"Peter Dickrell is Don Koch's second wife's father," Paula said.

"We can assume he's the owner of PD Holdings, but it's not listed here," Maddie said as she scrolled to Peter's employment history.

The report showed he'd spent the majority of his career with Control Data, a Bloomington-based firm that put Minnesota on the map as a leader in computer technology. He ascended the corporate ladder quickly. Then, according to the report, Peter co-founded a technology company, Dickrell-Kelly Research, with another former Control Data bigwig, Ethan Kelly.

"I remember my dad talking about this when he worked at Control Data," Paula said.

"That's right," Maddie said. "Your dad was an engineer there for many years."

"His entire career," Paula nodded. "Dickrell-Kelly was all over the news in the '90s. One of the founders bought the other out for millions. There were rumors about questionable business practices."

"Perhaps Peter Dickrell sold his shares, and it made him a very wealthy man," Maddie said. "What would compel him to get involved with his ex-son-in-law?"

"That's the multimillion-dollar question," Paula said.

Maddie and Paula gathered in Maddie's dining room with their friend Constance Lopez, studying the black and white images of the 1970 Cretin High School yearbook splayed open on the table. The senior boys in the photos had angular, smooth faces. Each donned a pressed white shirt and dark suit and tie. Young Victor Price wore black thick-rimmed glasses. He and the adolescent Addison and Brandon McGuinn had military haircuts. Teen-aged Don Koch's thick, dark hair was a little too long around his ears.

"I've done a lot of forensic accounting," Constance said. "I have never found anything like this."

Constance had worked as a special agent with the FBI for almost a decade. She had applied for the program at age 23, after working in local law enforcement for two years, and cleared the rigorous background investigation in just six months. Once she obtained her Top Secret/Sensitive Compartmented Information clearance and aced the physical fitness test multiple times, she worked as an agent on a reservation in northern Minnesota for two years and had her first pick of field offices. She chose the one in Brooklyn Center. Her fiance at the time was from Minneapolis and wanted to raise a family there. It felt close enough to home for Constance, who grew up in Chicago, so she agreed. The relationship didn't last, but Constance stayed in Minnesota and quickly became a star within the U.S. Department of Justice. She was recognized numerous times for her superior leadership skills and was selected to spearhead several investigations. She and Paula had worked on one such case a few years back, which was how they became friends. Eventually, Maddie began joining them for early morning breakfast meetups at a local diner. They occasionally met for dinner or drinks and had taken a couple of trips together.

"Who found these?" Constance asked.

"Simone, my ace paralegal," Maddie said, taking a long sip of red wine.

"Not in a million years would I have considered a high school connection," Paula said. She refilled her glass with what was left of the wine and held up the empty bottle. "Shall we have another?"

"Water for me," Constance said.

"It's a beautiful evening, let's move to the screened porch," Maddie said. She tossed the empty pizza box in the trash and opened a second bottle of wine.

As the women got settled into comfy chairs in the candlelit porch, the clear sapphire sky shifted to blue-black, and crickets noisily celebrated the darkness.

"I get the high school connection, but those guys all came from money, and they all went on to graduate from the top-tier universities," Maddie said. "Don attended Cretin on scholarship, skipped college and started selling cars right out of high school. Why do they remain so loyal to him?"

"Great question," Paula said.

"Have I mentioned Don is still pushing for the divorce to go to trial?" Maddie asked.

"That makes no sense," Paula said. "What's his motivation?"

"He claims it's about their daughter, Gabby," Maddie said.

Constance rolled her eyes. "That child would be better off without a father than with one like Don Koch."

"What can you tell me about the Peter Dickrell investigation?" Maddie asked, glancing back and forth between her friends.

"He works at Koch headquarters," Paula said. "He was brought on as a consultant around the time American Car Rental was purchased, managed the first wave of dealership closures, and he now oversees business operations."

"Does that include cooking the books?" Maddie asked.

Paula silently sipped her wine. Though the three of them often talked shop, some details of the criminal investigation could not be discussed with Maddie.

"How does it feel to be settled in your new home?" Constance asked, changing the subject.

"It feels like everything is finally falling into place," Maddie said.

"A toast to you and your beautiful house," Constance said, raising her glass.

"Yes!" Paula chimed in. "Cheers to your dream home!"

* * *

"There were at least a half-dozen men—and one woman—all wearing FBI jackets," Sue Primose said. Maddie switched the call to speaker mode as Simone positioned herself closer to listen. "They smashed out the glass in the door and carried out a computer and a printer,"

"Was anyone from PD Holdings on site?" Maddie asked.

"If you mean Mr. Mercedes, no, he hasn't been here," Sue said. "I haven't seen him since the day I sent you the photo of his license plate."

"Have you seen any reporters or members of the news media?" Maddie asked.

"No, I haven't," Sue said. "The FBI was on the premises for less than 30 minutes."

"What about your landlord?" Maddie asked.

"I left a voicemail, but he hasn't responded, and no one has been here to board up the broken window," Sue said.

Paula and Colin stood on the red stone plaza of the Diana E. Murphy U.S. Courthouse in the intense summer sun. Paula stepped up to the microphone to speak as dozens of journalists and cameras looked on.

"Earlier this week, the FBI executed a search and seizure on Don Koch's home and a number of businesses connected to the criminal case: Koch Automotive Group headquarters, several dealerships and PD Holdings. Based on evidence obtained in the search of those properties, a lawsuit was filed today against Peter Dickrell—a consultant for Koch Automotive Group—and his company, PD Holdings. It states, in part, that Mr. Dickrell began funneling money to Don Koch before Mr. Koch filed for bankruptcy. The intention of this arrangement, we believe, was to hide assets from the bankruptcy trustee and other creditors."

Reporters shifted in place anxiously as they waited for more details and an opening to ask questions.

"PD Holdings issued checks to a third party who provided an infusion of cash to Mr. Koch to cover personal expenses such golf course memberships, vacation properties and private school tuition for two of Mr. Koch's children, who happen to be Mr. Dickrell's grandchildren—" Paula paused to take a breath. "Peter Dickrell is the father of Don Koch's second wife, Tiffany Koch."

"Has Tiffany Koch been identified as a person of interest in the criminal case?" a reporter interrupted.

"Not at this time," Paula said, looking directly at the reporter.

* * *

Maddie sat in one of the chairs across from Paula and placed two paper-wrapped deli sandwiches on the desk between them. "Do you want egg salad or tuna salad?" she asked.

"Tuna," Paula said, passing a bottle of water to Maddie. "Thanks for coming to my office. I'd much rather be having lunch on a patio somewhere, but breaks for food feel like a luxury right now." The intercom on her desk phone buzzed. "Can it wait, Jenna?"

"I'm sorry to interrupt," Paula's legal secretary said. "Marilee Barber is on line three for you. She says it's urgent."

"Thanks, Jenna."

"Do you want me to step out?" Maddie asked.

Paula shook her head, took a deep breath and pressed the blinking button on her phone. "Hello, Marilee. What can I do for you?"

"I'm hoping we can have a constructive conversation about Addison and Brandon McGuinn," Marilee's voice crackled through the speaker.

CHAPTER TWENTY-FOUR

"What would you like to talk about?" Paula asked, unwrapping her sandwich. "A plea deal?"

"Frankly, I am astounded by the way my clients are being treated in this case," Marilee chided. "The McGuinn brothers are two of the most highly regarded businessmen in the state of Minnesota. In the U.S., for that matter. Don Koch is the criminal in this case."

"Marilee, as you are well aware, altering loan documents is a federal crime. And let's be real—birds of a feather flock together."

"What on earth are you talking about?"

"Don Koch and your clients have been friends since they were teenagers. They all went to high school together."

"That proves nothing," Marilee said.

"We have evidence your clients conspired with Don Koch to commit fraud. We have emails between Commonwealth Banc and Koch Automotive Group's former CFO, Richard Samuel, who was ordered to testify in federal court. We have proof of dozens of transactions for unsecured loans totaling millions of dollars."

"Bullshit!" Marilee barked.

"Marilee, unless your clients are interested in entertaining a plea deal and testifying against Don Koch, this conversation is pointless."

"The McGuinn brothers are innocent," Merilee fumed and disconnected the call.

"Marilee Barber is either in complete denial," Maddie said, looking down at her cell phone, which had just pinged with a text alert, "or she takes pleasure in representing the scum of the earth."

"Marilee is an attack dog, and she'll sink her teeth into whoever gets in her way," Paula said. She took a bite of her sandwich.

Maddie read the text message from Simone: "Have you seen this?" She clicked on the link, which led to video from a local news outlet. In the video, a reporter shouted, "Mr. Dickrell!" as she jogged toward him with her right arm extended, a microphone in her hand. "What's your response to the charges filed against you today?"

"No comment," he said. He walked swiftly toward an idling black Lincoln Town Car at the curb.

Before he reached the car, he was intercepted by a woman with a head of frizzy platinum blonde hair. "I hate you! I HATE YOU!" she shouted hoarsely, and slapped Peter's cheek.

Peter raised his left arm to shield his face as the woman continued flailing her fists at him frantically. He opened the back door of the waiting Town Car and slipped inside. The camera zoomed in on the blonde woman's face—her eyes were circled with black mascara and her body heaved as she cried.

"Holy shit," Maddie said, blinking in disbelief. "That's Tiffany Koch."

The languid days of summer were at their peak. Vegetable gardens were lush with produce. Sun worshippers and boaters cooled themselves in and around Minnesota's 10,000 lakes. Tourists explored the natural beauty and sights the state had to offer.

Maddie relished the quiet calm of a gorgeous morning as she sat in the screened porch with a cup of coffee and the newspaper. She flipped through the crisp pages of the Star Tribune, which had been delivered to her doorstep at the crack of dawn. As she considered refilling her coffee, she received a text alert from Paula who, like Maddie, preferred to read her news the old-fashioned way.

"Check out the first page of local section," the message said.

Maddie found the section and the headline she assumed Paula was referring to: "Abandoned sailboat found in Lake Minnetonka."

She continued reading:

"An unoccupied anchored sailboat was found Monday afternoon in Lake Minnetonka near Orono. Boaters discovered the sailboat with no one on board and notified authorities.

"According to the Hennepin County Sheriff's Office, the 35-foot coastal cruiser is registered to Peter Dickrell, whom sheriff's deputies have not been able to locate. A red Mercedes convertible registered to Dickrell was found in the parking lot of the Minnetonka Yacht Club, where law enforcement confirmed he has been a longtime member. For several years, he has participated in and won several sailing races hosted by the club.

"Water patrol was called to Crystal Bay late Monday and dive crews began to search the area. Crews have not discovered anything unusual. They will resume their search today.

"Dickrell is the father of Tiffany Koch, ex-wife of Twin Cities auto dealer Don Koch."

"What do you make of it?" Maddie texted Paula back.

As she waited for a response, she considered possible explanations for Peter's disappearance. Had he drowned by accident? It seemed unlikely given his experience as a sailor and the fact that the boat had been found anchored. Had he staged his own death and gone into hiding? Given his legal troubles, it certainly wasn't out of the question. Was there foul play? Was it possible Peter had been murdered? Did Don Koch have something to do with it?

The 10th largest body of water in Minnesota, Lake Minnetonka's maze of numerous interconnected bays and channels offered an abundance of majestic beauty that was ever-changing with the seasons. Its shores were home to local celebrities and old and new money alike, with stately mansions on sprawling lakefronts and meticulous boat houses dotting the shore.

CHAPTER TWENTY-FIVE

The lake's deepest waters were in Crystal Bay, where Peter's sailboat had been discovered. At 113 feet deep, it meant dive teams may not find Peter's remains, if there were any, for several days.

"Too soon to tell," Paula replied. "Breakfast at the diner?"

* * *

Maddie entered their regular breakfast spot 45 minutes later. She spotted Paula and Constance in their favorite corner booth. She slid in next to Constance and tucked her purse between them. "Good morning," she said. "Have you ordered?"

"Not yet," Constance said. She poured coffee from the carafe on the table into a white ceramic mug and pushed it toward Maddie.

"As I was saying," Paula addressed Constance. "He had a change of heart."

Maddie opened her menu. She scanned the breakfast selections, though she had the list memorized. She knew her friends were discussing Peter Dickrell and listened quietly.

"Had he changed his mind about his testimony?" Constance asked.

"The opposite," Paula said. "He claimed he had copies of falsified loan documents and agreed to turn them over. He admitted he bought into the scheme initially, and funneled money to his former son-in-law because he convinced him it was to help save the business, preserve some sort of legacy for his grandkids. After the raid, he realized he was being used."

A round waitress in an old-school diner uniform with "Bonnie" stitched above her right chest pocket seemed to appear out of nowhere. "Good morning ladies, what can I get you?" she asked.

"Just coffee for me," Paula said.

"Two eggs over easy with toast," Maddie said.

"I'll have the special," Constance said.

"You got it," Bonnie replied. She scribbled quickly on her pad, wedged her pen back to its home behind her right ear and collected the menus.

Paula lowered her voice. "A person who claimed to have direct evidence of Don Koch's criminal activity has disappeared and is likely dead," she said. "I doubt it's a coincidence."

Dawn White, attorney to Richard Samuel, the former Koch Automotive Group CFO who was ordered to testify in court, had requested an urgent meeting with Paula and Constance. The women cleared their schedules and agreed to meet at Paula's office. As they waited in the conference room and discussed emerging details in Don's criminal case, the 9 a.m. start time came and went.

"I hope we haven't been played," Constance said as she checked her watch again, a hint of irritation in her voice.

"Jenna—" Paula spoke into the spaceship-shaped speaker phone at the center of the conference table. "Will you see if you can reach Dawn White?"

"I'm on it," Jenna said. She called Paula back less than a minute later. "Her cell number is going to straight to voicemail."

At 9:22 a.m., just outside the small room where Paula and Constance waited, they overheard a woman speaking about construction on the freeway and rush hour traffic. Dawn walked into the room apologizing profusely. "I'm terribly sorry we're late," she said. "I should have allowed more time."

Directly behind the diminutive Dawn, Richard Samuel

entered. He was large but not obese—more big boned and solid, someone most men would avoid in a fist fight. His salt-and-pepper hair had more salt than pepper. The shadows around his eyes were prominent, as if he hadn't slept in days. He appeared uncomfortable in his navy blue suit and light blue button-down shirt, which was open at the collar.

Brief introductions were exchanged. Jenna brought Richard a cup of coffee and closed the door as she left.

Dawn pulled a file folder from her bag and placed it on the table. "I'll get right to the point," she said. "On Sunday evening, multiple rounds of bullets were fired at my client's residence. Mr. Samuel, his wife, and their three young children were home at the time. No one was physically injured or worse—thank god. Mr. Samuel believes his former employer, Don Koch, had something to do with the incident."

Constance glanced quickly at Paula. They knew that whatever information Richard was willing to provide was not purely out of the goodness of his heart; he was there to strike a deal.

"Mr. Samuel, before you say anything, we have to ask you—are you willing to testify in a court of law?" Paula asked.

Richard looked over at Dawn and slid his coffee mug to the side. "Yes, I am," he said.

He took a deep breath and continued. "Our house is on the corner. I was grilling burgers in the backyard. My daughters were playing on the swings. My wife came outside with our 10-month-old and told the girls to go in the house to wash their hands. As I looked up from the grill, a black SUV turned the corner and stopped. Suddenly, the windows lowered, there were guns pointed at the house, bullets were flying everywhere. I yelled at my wife to get down and ran to the girls to get them down on the ground. The SUV was gone in a matter of seconds." Richard paused, looked at the ceiling and blinked back tears. A weighty silence filled the air.

"The vehicle was found abandoned less than three miles from the Samuels' home and it was identified as stolen," Dawn said.

"What makes you think Don Koch was behind it?" Constance asked.

"Special Agent Lopez, you know as well as I do, if the perpetrators of this crime were shooting to kill, my client wouldn't be sitting here today," Dawn said. "This was to send a message."

"What message?" Paula asked.

"To keep my mouth shut," Richard said.

"As its former CFO, Mr. Samuel has evidence about Koch Automotive Group's business practices that could be crucial to the criminal case," Dawn said.

"We're listening," Paula said.

Dawn placed a palm on the folder on the table. "Mr. Samuel can provide copies of more than 100 documents, including the original loan agreement for Koch Automotive Group's purchase of American Car Rental, and altered documents used to secure millions in financing from Freedom Financial to purchase vehicles for American Car Rental."

"Only the funds were never used to purchase vehicles," Richard said. "Don used the money to maintain the lifestyle he's accustomed to, and to pay off the people who know what he's up to."

"People like you?" Paula asked.

Richard pursed his lips and looked down at the table.

"Mr. Samuel," Constance said, "How did you gain access to these documents?"

Richard shifted in his chair. "Koch Automotive Group used to be a great place to work. For years, Don and I were like brothers. There was a drastic shift in his behavior around the time of the American Car Rental deal—it was erratic. He was unable to focus. He was easily distracted. He jumped from one deal to the next. While he was staying at his vacation property in California, he asked me to email a document that he had saved on his desktop computer at the office. While I was searching for it, I came across correspondence with an overseas pharmaceutical company about purchasing Oxytocin. There were also documents that detailed several high stakes bets he'd placed. I was stunned."

"To your knowledge, does Mr. Koch use or sell drugs?" Constance asked.

"I thought it might explain his odd behavior, but I honestly don't know."

"You had no knowledge of his gambling?" Constance asked.

"I had no idea," Richard said, and tugged his ear. "Not long after that, he asked me to falsify invoices, and a short time later, loan documents."

"And you agreed?" Paula asked.

"He's one hell of a salesman," Richard said and paused. "He

convinced me it was a short-term solution to the company's cash flow problems."

"Mr. Samuel," Constance said, her tone sardonic. "Surely you knew what you were doing was illegal. What was in it for you?"

He cleared his throat. "Don was the force behind the company's success for years. He rewarded his leadership team handsomely."

"Are you indebted to Mr. Koch?" Constance asked.

"Not financially, if that's what you mean. If you're asking if has something over me, the answer is no. There is a dark side of Don that only a select few have witnessed. If he thinks someone has betrayed him, he can be ruthless. A decade ago, he terminated a long-time employee, Trey Calvers, who he was sure was embezzling from the company. Trey had been his right-hand man for years. After he fired him, Don made Trey's life hell. I watched that situation unfold and realized Don will do whatever he deems necessary to get revenge. It occurred to me that I might need an insurance policy to protect myself someday. I started making copies of the illegal transactions."

"Please give us specifics about the documents you are prepared to turn over, Mr. Samuel," Constance said.

"There are copies of original and altered versions of correspondence, invoices and loan documents that were sent to Freedom Financial and other automotive financial institutions over a two-year period."

"The evidence will need to be evaluated," Paula said.

"Of course," Dawn said. "As you are no doubt aware, Mr. Samuel is putting himself at great risk by sharing this information. His safety must be central to any deal. He is willing to provide this evidence in exchange for full immunity." She looked directly at Constance. "The Federal Witness Protection Program is crucial for Mr. Samuel and his family."

The Edina Police Department had no solid leads on the gunmen who had targeted Richard Samuel. At the crime scene, they had collected more than 80 bullet casings from two different firearms—a Glock 40 and a Smith & Wesson 9 mm. The SUV had been reported stolen in Minneapolis the day before the shooting and was found not long after the incident. It contained no weapons or any other conclusive evidence.

A break in the case came when one of the assailants, a career criminal in Illinois, posted a video of himself on social media waving a Glock pistol and a wad of cash, boasting that he'd scored "$50K for having a little fun at a backyard barbecue two states away." Two days later, the Chicago man, Antonio Duran, and two men thought to be his accomplices were extradited to Minnesota by U.S. Marshals. Ballistics on weapons confiscated during their arrests were a match to those used at the shooting outside the Samuels' home.

Transcripts of the interrogation between detectives and the alleged shooters revealed they had been hired by a "white dude known as 'Million Dollar Bill.'" Antonio claimed they were paid $25,000 cash from "Bill" up front, which they collected at Navy Pier, and another $25,000, which was handed off in a rest stop parking lot in DeKalb after the job was done.

* * *

"Good morning, Cummins Law Office," Simone answered the phone. "Hello, Sue," she said warmly. "Yes, she's at her desk. Just a moment."

Maddie overheard Simone from her office. "Sue Primrose?" she deduced.

"Yes," Simone said. "She tried your cell phone and got voicemail. She says it's urgent. She sounds upset."

"Hi Sue," Maddie said into the handset. "Is everything OK?"

Tripping over her words, Sue informed Maddie that she'd been watching the morning news when a "WANTED BY THE FBI" graphic with the image of a man who looked exactly like her landlord appeared on the screen.

"You're 100 percent certain?" Maddie asked.

"Yes, I'm sure," Sue said.

"Hold tight and I will call you back," Maddie said. "Keep your phone nearby."

"OK," Sue said.

"What was that all about?" Simone asked, standing in the doorway of Maddie's office.

"Sue identified a man on an FBI wanted poster as William Parker," she said. "Do you have photo you found when you were researching Commercial Pros?"

"I'm sure I do," Simone said. She disappeared from the doorway.

As Simone rummaged through a stack of papers on her desk, Maddie opened her cell phone and selected Constance's number in her contact list.

"Hi, Maddie," Constance said after one ring.

"Hey," Maddie said as Simone handed her the photo of William from the Commercial Pros webpage. She placed it on the desk next to a printout of the grainy image of the "wanted" man from the FBI's website. "There was a story on the news this morning about a search for a man connected to a drive-by shooting in Edina."

"Yes," Constance said.

"Remember the State Farm agent whose office is in the same business center as PD Holdings, Sue Primose?"

"Yes."

"She just called to say the man on the poster is her landlord, William Parker," Maddie said.

The chill of autumn had settled in. Maddie had succeeded in invalidating the Kochs' prenuptial agreement based on Don's failure to disclose assets, but doing so hadn't made drafting a settlement agreement simpler. In fact, quite the opposite. It had been extremely difficult to create a legitimate list of marital assets. Once they had, every settlement offer proposed regarding the distribution of those assets was rejected by Don. He was also hung up on the proposed shared custody of their daughter. After many months of negotiations with no end in sight, Jayne had finally reached her limit.

"He doesn't care about Gabby," she insisted. "He only cares about money."

Ready to be free of Don once and for all, Jayne proposed an agreement that was far from typical. Maddie wasn't sure it would work, but if Jayne was right, if Don cared more about money than his child, the most contentious divorce case she'd ever taken on would finally be settled.

The meeting was set to take place at the Gold and Stein offices, a conciliatory gesture Maddie hoped would not go unnoticed. The women made small talk in the car as Maddie drove them downtown to the appointment.

"I don't think I mentioned how I got my great-grandmother's necklace back—the one Don said he took to a jeweler to have professionally cleaned," Jayne said. She untwisted the seatbelt over her coral-colored linen suit.

"No, I don't think you did," Maddie said, her eyes on the road.

"When the appraiser discovered some of the stones had been replaced with fakes, I thought the jeweler who cleaned it may have stolen them, so I hired a private investigator. He found the stones had been sold to a dealer, and the person who sold them to the dealer was my hustling husband. Miraculously, the dealer still had the stones."

"Wow," Maddie said, astounded. "Did you buy them back?"

"I would have, they mean that much to me," Jayne said. "In the end, Don paid for them."

"How?" Maddie asked. She turned her head briefly to take in Jayne's self-righteous smile.

"I pilfered from Don's collection of watches and cuff links and exchanged them for my great-grandmother's jewels," Jayne said. "I had the necklace refurbished and moved it to a safe at the bank."

"Don hasn't noticed the missing Rolexes?" Maddie asked. She wondered what it might be like to own so many expensive watches that you didn't notice your collection had dwindled.

Jayne's hair grazed her shoulders as she shook her head. "Nope."

Gold and Stein's elaborate offices were located on an upper floor of the Wells Fargo Bank tower in Minneapolis. Elizabeth greeted Maddie and Jayne in the dark wood-paneled lobby and led them to a private conference room off a dimly lit hallway. Don paced in the corner of the room, his cell phone pressed firmly to his ear. He didn't seem to notice he was no longer alone. He wore a gray suit with light-colored pinstripes. A red silk tie and matching pocket square accented his attire. His hair was, as always, in need of a good cut.

"Mr. Koch, we're ready to begin," Elizabeth said, closing the door behind her.

Don gave a single nod in Elizabeth's direction and continued his phone conversation. Without warning, Jayne grabbed her Louis Vuitton purse by the strap and flung it onto the conference table. As the bag met the table with a thump, everyone in the room jumped.

"Hang up the phone NOW," Jayne demanded. "We are settling this divorce TODAY."

Elizabeth smiled nervously.

Don disconnected the call and slid his phone into his pocket. "Calm down—"

"TODAY," Jayne reiterated and turned to Maddie.

Maddie took a deep breath. "Mr. Koch, it's in everyone's best interest to put an end to this impasse. Given your mounting legal issues, we would like to propose an unconventional settlement."

"What do you mean, unconventional?" Don said.

Maddie passed Elizabeth and Don each a multi-page document that outlined the agreement. "Ms. Koch is prepared to buy out your child support obligations, Mr. Koch, in exchange for the termination of your parental rights to your child, Gabrielle Koch—"

"No fucking way," Don said, his eyes bulging. "Gabby is my flesh and blood."

"Oh, please," Jayne scoffed. "Since we separated, you've seen her twice for a total of two hours and 40 minutes."

Elizabeth scanned the document and blinked rapidly when she reached the section with the proposed cash offer, which was just shy of $5 million.

Don flipped back and forth between the pages of the document. "All this time you've been arguing about the prenup and marital assets," he said. "And you're the one who's been doing the hiding."

"As your attorney will attest, Mr. Koch, an inheritance that was awarded before marriage and has remained in a separate account is not marital property," Maddie said. "Not only was Ms. Koch not required to include it on the list of assets, she was not obligated to tell you about it."

Elizabeth primly folded her perfectly manicured hands and placed them on the table. "Mr. Koch and I will need to discuss the proposed settlement privately," she announced. "If you wouldn't mind waiting in the lobby."

Maddie settled into a brown leather chair in the spacious lobby while Jayne stepped into the entryway to make a phone call. Fifteen minutes later, just as Jayne returned and took a seat in the chair next to Maddie, Elizabeth appeared at the hallway entrance and invited them back to the conference room.

Don had opened the button at his collar and loosened his tie. He avoided eye contact with Jayne and Maddie and looked directly at his attorney.

"This is an intriguing offer," Elizabeth said. "We're going to need some additional time to thoroughly review the document."

"You have 72 hours," Maddie said. "After that, the agreement is void."

"I'm sorry I've had to reschedule twice," Maddie said. She removed the plastic lid from her latte and blew on the drink. "I'm overloaded with cases at the moment. I only have a few minutes to chat."

"I completely understand," Hazel said, tucking her long bangs behind her ear. "I'm grateful to you for taking the time to meet again."

Behind Hazel's stylish glasses, Maddie detected a sparkle in her eyes and a sprinkling of pale freckles across her cheeks and nose that she hadn't noticed during their first meeting. It occurred to her that Hazel looked nothing like Don, and exactly like a younger version her mother, Lisa. "You mentioned in your message you were offered a family law internship," Maddie said. "Tell me about it."

Hazel nodded as she took a bite of her chocolate croissant. "With West Metro Family Law—do you know anything about them?"

"Yes," Maddie said. "They're one of the most successful firms in town."

"That's what I've heard, but I'm a little worried," Hazel said.

"What worries you?" Maddie asked.

"Frankly," Hazel said, "there are no women or people of color working at the firm."

"That's true," Maddie acknowledged. "They are not known for being a diverse group."

"Seems like a bit of an old boys club," Hazel said. "I am not interested in being the token female member."

"I get it," Maddie said. "If something is telling you it's not a good fit, it probably isn't. You're at the top of your class. More opportunities will surely come your way."

Hazel shared details about a few other firms that were on her radar. Maddie mentioned a half-dozen more that were reputable and worth reaching out to.

"I don't know why," Hazel said, "I thought you were going to tell me I should take the position at West Metro."

"Hell no!" Maddie said. "I am a firm believer in trusting your gut."

"Me too," Hazel said. "I'm getting better at it, thanks to my therapist, Samantha."

"That reminds me—thank you for referring me to Samantha," Maddie said. "We spoke on the phone last week, and I shared details about recurring nightmares I've been having since experiencing transient global amnesia. She explained the TGA may have caused an emotional upheaval that is bringing memories to the surface. We're meeting in a couple of weeks to try hypnosis, to see if I recover some of my memories."

"I'm glad you connected; I hope she can help," Hazel said.

CHAPTER TWENTY-NINE

"I hope so, too," Maddie said. "Though I have to admit, what those buried memories might reveal is a bit daunting."

Maddie contemplated sharing what Samantha had said about the events leading up to her TGA episode, how it was possible her very survival had been at stake during that time, and that the nightmares could be one of her body's ways of working through the trauma.

"I get it," Hazel said, before Maddie could say more. "Working with her has been one of the most difficult things I have done in my life, but it has been worthwhile."

Maddie wondered if Hazel might expand on her experience. She thought about asking if the repressed memories she had uncovered had something to do with what she'd said last time they met, about growing up with a father who had no morals.

"So—" Hazel said, filling the silence. "I heard Don Koch relinquished parental rights to his youngest daughter in exchange for $5 million."

This caught Maddie off guard. "Pardon me?" she replied.

"Jayne and I talk often. She wants Gabby to have a relationship with her sisters. I love that little girl so much."

"Of course," Maddie said. She wondered why she hadn't considered it sooner. There would always be a biological connection between Don's children.

"She's better off without him," Hazel said.

"You're not the first person to say so," Maddie said. Her thoughts drifted to her own father, his unexpected passing more than a decade ago, and how she'd do anything to have him back again.

"I hope I didn't overstep," Hazel said, noticing a shift in Maddie's mood.

"No, no." Maddie shook her head and gathered her things. "My mind is already on my next meeting. I have to get going."

They stood and made their way outside to the sidewalk outside the coffee shop.

"Great to see you again," Hazel said, giving Maddie a quick hug.

"You, too. I'll ask around. Someone in my network might be in need of an intern. I'll reach out if I hear of anything."

"I've discovered another unbelievable Koch connection," Simone announced as Maddie walked into the office. She held out a copy of what appeared to be an old newspaper article.

Maddie set her purse and briefcase on one of the chairs in lobby, took the paper from Simone and read the headline aloud: "Cretin hockey primed for a playoff run led by record-setting goalie." She paused as she glanced up at Simone and continued. "The Cretin hockey team will take on Edina Wednesday night in the section semifinals. The section is as tough as it gets with Minneapolis Southwest the No. 1 seed and Cretin the No. 2 seed. If these teams win on Wednesday, they'll meet Friday night for a spot in the state tournament.

"The 1969-1970 season has been a record breaker for Cretin, thanks in part to the boys known as the 'Cretin Six,' a core group of players who have shared the ice for four seasons, and in some cases even longer. The star of the team is senior goaltender, Frank Larson, who last month became the all-time winningest netminder in Minnesota State High School League history, notching his 90th save. The group also includes forwards Addison McGuinn, Brandon McGuinn and Victor Price, and defensive players Don Koch and William—" Maddie shook her head in disbelief. "William Parker?"

Simone nodded. "I know what you're thinking. William Parker was not in the Cretin yearbook."

"Exactly," Maddie said.

"In theory, his senior picture should have been right here with the others," Simone said. She handed Maddie the book open to the spread of pages with tiled images they'd examined several times—all boys with last names starting with letters K through P.

"Koch, McGuinn, McGuinn, Price," Maddie said, tapping each of the four photos.

"Well, apparently young William Parker was absent on picture day," Simone said and flipped to the back of the book. "He's listed here, on the 'not pictured' page."

"Incredible," Maddie said. She snapped a photo of the yearbook page and texted it to Paula with a note that said, "Another Cretin connection."

"What about Frank Larson?" Maddie asked. "That's a name we haven't heard."

"One step ahead of you," Simone said, flipping to a page near the front of the yearbook. A candid photo of a handsome young man smiling broadly for the camera filled most of the page. Above the image were the words "In Memoriam," and below the photo, "Francis (Frank) Larson" and "1952-1970."

"Take a look at this," Simone said, handing Maddie a copy of another old newspaper article. Under the Duluth News

CHAPTER THIRTY

Tribune masthead was the headline: "Boot of missing teen found after storm."

"What the—" Maddie said, skimming the article.

"I searched for an obituary for Frank Larson. I couldn't find one, but I did find a missing persons report," Simone said. She handed over a copy of the handwritten report from the Duluth Police Department.

"Summarize it for me," Maddie said.

"The 'Cretin Six' took a road trip to Duluth to meet Olympic Gold Medal-winning hockey player Tommy 'The Bomber' Wilson, who played for the Minnesota North Stars at the time. Tommy grew up in Duluth and had a big house there with an outdoor rink. Frank's dad had a connection and arranged for the boys to spend a day on the ice with Tommy. After skating for several hours, the boys went to buy groceries and liquor and headed to the shores of Lake Superior where they planned to roast hot dogs. The made a fire on the beach, but it was much colder there than they thought it would be, so they headed to the Lake View Motel, a few blocks from the lake. Frank's mother had booked two adjoining rooms for the six of them. At some point after that, Frank went missing. The next morning, after searching for their friend for a couple of hours, Addison called the Duluth Police Department. All five boys were interviewed by the police and provided statements. Frank's parents arrived that afternoon and filed an official report. Their son was never found."

"I'm calling Paula and Constance," Maddie said. She selected Paula's number in her contacts, and it went directly to voicemail.

The same thing happened when she pressed Constance's number. She sent a text in their group chat: "Call me ASAP."

"These men have a history together that is much more complicated than anyone could have imagined," Simone said.

Two days after Peter Dickrell's sailboat was found abandoned on Lake Minnetonka, the Hennepin County Sheriff's Dive Team recovered his body from the lake. Officials suspected foul play and an autopsy was being performed.

Bernard Gold, who was in the process of negotiating a plea deal on behalf of Don, dropped him as a client. When it came to retaining new counsel, despite the multimillion-dollar settlement he was awarded in the dissolution of his marriage with Jayne, Don claimed he could not afford an attorney. The court appointed a public defender. Shortly after, the prosecution informed the public defender that a deal was off the table—Don's case would go to trial.

Though her official dealings with Don had concluded, Maddie's preoccupation with his sordid past and the criminal case continued. Still, she had other clients to focus on. She was only half listening to the TV news while she sorted through Simone's notes relating to a new case.

"This just in," anchorman Dan Selby said. "The Hennepin County Coroner's Office released the autopsy report for Peter Dickrell."

Maddie grabbed the remote and turned up the volume.

"Dickrell's unoccupied sailboat was found anchored in Lake Minnetonka's Crystal Bay on Aug. 12. Dickrell's body was discovered by the Hennepin County Sheriff's Dive Team on Aug. 14; his death appeared to be an accident. Medical examiners have ruled Dickrell's death a homicide. Angie Jones joins us from the Noerenberg Memorial Gardens nature preserve with more details."

The shot cut away from the studio to a reporter standing in the nature preserve's parking lot with a large Hennepin County Sheriff Mobile Command Center truck directly behind her. "That's right, Dan, medical examiners have ruled Peter Dickrell's death a homicide based on two key findings." The reporter looked down at her notes and then directly into the camera. "There was air in his lungs, which indicates he was dead before his body entered the water. Additionally, Dickrell experienced a blunt-force trauma to the back of his skull, which the medical examiner confirmed was the cause of death. Based on the shape and size of the wound, it was likely the result of being struck by a claw hammer.

"Earlier today, divers returned to the waters of Crystal Bay to search for a possible murder weapon. The dive team concluded their search a short while ago, just before sundown. They were not successful in retrieving any additional evidence today." Angie swiveled her hips toward the vehicle behind her. "As you can see, they've set up a mobile command center on-site; they will resume their search tomorrow morning. Since the death was officially ruled a homicide, the Hennepin County Sheriff's Office is asking for the public's help. Please call the number on the screen if you have any information you think might be helpful in this investigation."

Maddie stared motionless at the television and absorbed the details.

"Thank you, Angie," Dan Selby said, looking directly into the camera. "Stay tuned to WCCO TV. We will continue to update you on this story as details become available."

* * *

Just after 6 the next morning, Bonnie welcomed Maddie as she entered the diner. An older gentleman seated alone at the counter with a plate of half-eaten eggs and toast looked briefly in her direction. He smiled and turned his attention back to the newspaper he was reading. A young couple who appeared to have been out celebrating all night huddled in a booth talking quietly.

"Good morning, Bonnie," Maddie said, heading toward the corner booth. "Am I the first to arrive?"

"Yup," Bonnie confirmed as she shuffled over to the table with a carafe of coffee, her orthopedic shoes squeaking on the glossy checkerboard tiles. Maddie turned a white ceramic mug upright on its saucer. Bonnie filled it and asked, "Would you like to order, or do you want to wait?"

"I'll give them a few minutes," Maddie said. "Any specials today?"

"Steak and eggs," Bonnie said, leaving the carafe on the table. "Holler if you need me."

Whenever they met for breakfast, Paula and Constance almost always arrived at the restaurant before Maddie. With the announcement of Peter's autopsy results the evening before, she assumed the two of them were knee-deep in the case. Maddie's work in family law rarely crossed over into Paula's territory, and she had never been involved in a federal case. Though she and Simone had played a role in discovering evidence key to Don's criminal investigation, there were limits to what Paula and Constance could share with her about the federal case. Maddie understood this, and yet she found herself experiencing something she hadn't before—the feeling she was missing out. She pulled her phone from her bag and checked the messages. There were no new texts or voicemails.

"Still on for breakfast?" she typed in their group text and then opened the Minnesota Public Radio website. She scrolled through the news headlines. Peter's murder was among the top stories, but there were no additional details that hadn't already been announced.

The bell on the door jingled. Paula and Constance entered and sat across from Maddie in the booth. She poured each of them a cup of coffee and refilled her own. "I thought I might be eating breakfast solo this morning," she said.

"This may be the only meal I have a chance to eat today," Paula said, carefully sipping the scalding liquid.

"Any new developments since the autopsy results were released?" Maddie inquired.

"The dive team resumes the search for a potential murder weapon this morning," Constance said, looking at the menu. "Law enforcement is looking into a tip that was called in by a member of the Lafayette Club who was on the golf course and saw the boat and people on it."

Bonnie reappeared with her green pad and ballpoint pen in hand. "Morning, ladies," she acknowledged Constance and Paula. "Ready to order?"

"Good morning, Bonnie," Paula said. "I'd like fresh fruit and yogurt, please."

"I'll have the steak and eggs special," Maddie said. "Steak medium, eggs over easy."

"That sounds good," Constance said. "I'll have the same."

"Got it," Bonnie said, lifting the now empty carafe from the table and giving it a shake. "More coffee?"

"Yes, please," Maddie said. She paused and addressed Constance. "Sue Primrose asked me to bring her to your office this week," she said.

"Did you tell her I won't bite?" Constance asked.

"Yes," Maddie chuckled. "I assured her it was just a formality."

"Can we just take a moment to again acknowledge Simone's investigative work," Paula said. "The details she uncovered about the Cretin Six—"

"Incredible," Constance said.

"She really is the best," Maddie acknowledged. "I'm hoping she'll take the bar exam in February and join the firm as a partner."

"That would be amazing," Paula said.

"The two of you would make quite the dynamic duo," Constance said.

As the women continued the conversation, Bonnie returned with plates of steak and eggs and a bowl of plain yogurt topped with berries. The three of them dug into their breakfast, and Maddie shared details about her recent meeting with Don's daughter, Hazel.

"She was offered an internship at West Metro Family Law, but she's going to turn it down," Maddie said.

"Based on something you said?" Paula asked.

"No, I told her it was one of the most successful family law practices in town," Maddie said. "She noticed the lack of diversity there and decided to hold out for a firm that's more inclusive."

"Good for her," Paula said.

"I'm not sure that would have occurred to me at her age," Constance said.

"She has a great head on her shoulders," Maddie said.

"Hard to believe she's Don's daughter," Paula said.

Constance nodded as she chewed a forkful of steak.

"It's clear she wants nothing to do with him," Maddie said. "She legally changed her last name to her mother's maiden name."

"You mentioned that after you first met," Paula said.

"Did I also mention I had a conversation with Samantha, the therapist who helped Hazel work through repressed memories from her childhood?"

CHAPTER THIRTY-ONE

"No," Paula said, wiping her mouth with a napkin. "Say more."

"Hazel hasn't said anything specific about the memories she recovered, just that the process was difficult. She thought her therapist could potentially help me with my memory loss, so I scheduled an appointment."

"At the ER, Dr. Englund said the memories lost during an episode of TGA are typically lost forever," Paula said.

"Typically, yes," Maddie said. "But it's worth a try."

While she waited for Maddie and Sue to arrive, Constance reviewed surveillance video footage from Navy Pier and the DeKalb rest area on a large monitor mounted on the wall of the interview room. She'd examined the footage dozens of times at her desk, always searching for additional details she may have missed.

In the video captured at Navy Pier on Sept. 6, Antonio Duran and his two associates were clearly recognizable. As was the man they interacted with. An image of the fourth man was pulled from this video and broadcast by local television stations on behalf of the FBI; it was the image Sue had seen when she contacted Maddie.

The suspects in the video date-stamped Sept.7—the date of the drive-by shooting at former Koch Automotive Group CFO Richard Samuel's Edina residence—were more difficult to discern. Constance rewound to the 11:27 p.m. time marker. The footage was captured from a camera mounted inside the entrance of a single-story building that housed public restrooms, a sprawling rack of tourism brochures, and an alcove with at least a dozen vending machines. A middle-aged white male with a black baseball cap and a younger blonde woman in a denim skirt entered the building together. She walked swiftly to the women's room. He meandered into the men's room. Five minutes later, he exited the restroom, drank from the water fountain mounted on the wall, and left the building. The blonde exited the women's room at 11:45 p.m. and sat on a bench in the waiting area near the vending machines. She removed her phone from her purse and began typing.

From a camera perched atop a light pole in the parking lot, video captured minutes earlier, at 11:15 p.m., showed the blonde woman climbing into the cab of a parked semitrailer, and shortly after, exiting the truck and entering the building with the man in the black cap. At 11:32 p.m., the man left the building and returned to his truck without the woman. A few minutes later, at 11:44 p.m., he drove off.

As the truck exited, a white SUV with no license plates and windows tinted so dark it was impossible to see inside the vehicle pulled into the lot. The woman in the rest stop building looked up from her phone, stood quickly, and scurried into the women's room.

It was almost midnight when a black Lincoln Navigator, also without plates, pulled into the lot. Two men got out of the white vehicle from the front and back passenger's side and approached the driver's side of the black SUV. Through the Navigator's windshield, which was not tinted, the outline of a man could be seen tendering a package to the men. The man was not recognizable. It was too dark, and the video was too grainy.

Constance paused the video and glanced at her watch. It

was almost time to meet Maddie and Sue in the lobby. As she rewound the video, a flash on the monitor caught her eye. She examined the screen closely. For just a second, a rectangular object on the front passenger seat of the Navigator reflected the glow of a high mast light in the parking lot.

"Is that a license plate?" Constance said to herself. She reached for the remote, rewound the video again and enlarged the image on the screen.

It was a license plate. Only the lower third of the letters and numbers on the plate were visible. But along the bottom, in bold black print as clear as day, was the word "dealer." It was a dealer registration plate, the kind used on vehicles that auto dealerships own and offer for sale.

* * *

"I'm nervous," Sue admitted to Maddie as they entered the squatty security building just outside the black iron fence that surrounded the FBI field office.

"Nothing to be nervous about," Maddie assured her. "You're just going to review some video footage."

"The security clearance form was a little intimidating," Sue said. "I sure do appreciate you being here with me."

An officer in the security building checked them in. "You'll need to leave your cell phones and laptops here," he directed. "Special Agent Lopez will meet you in the lobby of the main building."

In the lobby, a giant screen featured images of the FBI's

10 most wanted fugitives. Constance approached the women as they entered, nodded at Maddie, and extended her hand to Sue. "I'm Special Agent Lopez," she said warmly. "Thank you for taking the time to be here today. For each step Constance and Maddie took, Sue took two. She struggled to keep up as they walked quickly toward the tired-looking sprawling government building.

Just before they reached the elevator bank, Maddie noticed Sue was out of breath. "Need a minute?" she asked.

"What I need is to quit smoking," Sue said with a chortle. "I'm fine."

Constance led them to the meeting room on the fourth floor. "Can I get either of you something to drink?" she asked.

"No, thank you," Maddie said, taking a seat facing the monitor on the wall.

"Nothing for me, thanks," Sue said, sitting next to Maddie.

"As you know, Ms. Primrose, you're here because you believe you can identify a man from an image captured on surveillance video who is a suspect in a federal crime," Constance said.

"Out of curiosity, do you get a lot of calls from these types of photos?" Sue asked.

"Yes, we do," Constance said. "Though they are not always helpful."

"I hope I'm not wasting your time," Sue said.

After a brief explanation, Constance played the surveillance footage from Navy Pier. A large Ferris wheel loomed in the background. Antonio and his two associates stood at the pier's edge overlooking Lake Michigan. Antonio wore a hooded sweatshirt and a Chicago White Sox baseball cap. A fit, older man with jet black hair strode toward them. He wore jeans and a light-colored jacket.

"That's my landlord!" Sue said immediately. "That's definitely William Parker!"

William appeared to survey his surroundings as he approached the three men. Antonio nodded and stepped forward; he and William engaged in conversation. All four men walked the length of the pier together until they were out of the camera's view.

In the next video, captured from a different camera, the group of men walked past the Navy Pier Auditorium. They stopped at the pier's end, a few feet from the water. Constance paused the video on the frame that had been used for the "wanted" poster and enlarged it, so William's face was featured prominently on the screen.

"You're 100 percent certain this man is William Parker?" Constance asked.

"Yes," Sue said, emphatically. "His hair, his build, the way he walks—it's him."

Constance didn't share the remaining portion of the video with Sue. In it, William removed a small package from inside his jacket and handed it to Antonio. Antonio looked inside the package. One of his associates lifted his T-shirt to reveal a gun tucked into the waistband of his jeans. William backed away and raised his hands slightly. Antonio stashed the package in his sweatshirt pocket. The group of three turned and walked into the terminal. William went the opposite direction, sauntering back down the pier.

FEBRUARY 1970

Night had fallen, the sky was pitch-black, and stars twinkled like jewels against the darkness. Addison, Brandon, Don, Frank, Victor and William stood in their snowmobile boots around a blazing fire they'd made on the snow-packed shores of Lake Superior. The temperature in Duluth had been in the 20s and sunny earlier—perfect for playing hockey outside with their idol, former Olympic gold medalist and current Minnesota North Star center Tommy Wilson. After the sun had gone down, the temp had plummeted to zero. They were hearty Minnesota stock, accustomed to the cold, and most of them had dressed for the weather with L.L.Bean down jackets and snow pants. Except for Don, who had borrowed his dad's two-sizes-too-big motor oil-stained brown insulated Carhartt coveralls.

"Today may have been the best day of my life," Frank said, his huge smile aglow in the firelight.

"Same here," Addison said. "Your dad is the best for setting it up."

"Guys, look!" Victor said, pointing toward the lake. "The Northern Lights!"

Suddenly, the clear dark sky transformed into rivers of

greenish-blue light that swirled in the sky above them. The solar wind and the earth's magnetic field had begun to dance, their movements unpredictable, sometimes barely perceptible, and then suddenly voluminous and vivid again.

"Far out!" William said.

The others chimed in with, "Whoa!" and "Cool!"

Don stood silently and took a long pull from his beer. "You're all a bunch of girls," he said brusquely.

"At least us girls can afford snow pants," Frank said, and all the boys laughed.

"Fuck you, Frank!" Don said, slamming his bottle to the ground. He clenched his fists and puffed up his chest.

Addison held Don back. "Take it easy, man," he said. "It was a joke."

"He is always talking shit about my family," Don said, kicking the bottle into the fire. "I'm sick of it."

"No, he's not," Brandon said, putting his arm around Don.

"Seriously, man," William said. He began to sing: "We're the Cretin Six!"

The rest of the boys joined in, "We're the Cretin Six! We're the Cretin Six! Whether we're on the ice or off the ice, together we will stick!" They repeated the chant again and again, louder and louder each time. They lifted their bottles and clanked them together. Don and Frank hugged.

For what felt like hours, they drank beer, talked about hockey and their plans for the future. When the beer was gone, they passed around a fifth of Jack Daniels and roasted hot dogs on sticks. Everyone had a buzz, but Don and Frank were obviously more intoxicated than the others.

"I gotta piss," Don announced and stumbled forward. He almost fell into the dying flames.

"Careful, big guy," Addison said and pulled him back.

Don swayed. He took the final gulp of Jack Daniels and threw the bottle into the embers. Then he fell flat on his ass. The group roared with laughter.

"Don's drunk!" Victor said.

"Good luck getting your old man's coveralls off before you piss yourself," Frank jeered.

Don stood and charged at Frank, tackling him. The two awkwardly tussled on the ground for a minute before the others pulled them apart and up on their feet.

"Knock it off! William said.

"It's after midnight, the fire's dead, and it's fucking freezing," Addison said. "Let's go to the motel."

"Where's my boot?" Frank said. He looked down at his right foot clad only in a ragg wool sock.

"Jesus, Frank," William said.

"Brand-new Sorels," Frank said. "My dad's gonna kill me."

"C'mon guys, let's pick up the trash and look for Frank's boot," Addison said.

As they clumsily gathered the empty whiskey and beer bottles, Don announced, "I found your fucking boot, asshole," and held it in the air. "Now go and get it!" He flung the boot out onto the icy lake where it landed with a dull thump.

"What the fuck, Don? Why would you do that?" William said.

Frank stumbled toward the lake.

"Don't walk out on the ice!" Addison said.

"Relax," Don said. "It's frozen solid."

"We'll come back tomorrow during the daylight and get it," Addison said.

The wind picked up and howled across the lake. The six of them trudged up the steep hill from the shore toward the Lake View Motel. Addison and William led, followed by Don, Brandon and Victor. Frank lagged in the back, limping on his bootless foot.

* * *

Sunlight floated into the large front window of the motel room. Addison was the first of the group to wake, blurry-eyed and hungover. As his vision adjusted, he checked the clock—it was almost 7 a.m. His roommates, Brandon and William, were sound asleep in the pair of double beds. Heavy snoring from the adjoining room was amplified in his throbbing head. He rose from the sofa bed where he'd been sleeping to shut the door between the two rooms. He quickly realized something was amiss. Victor and Don were asleep in the double beds in the other room, but the pull-out bed was still folded into a sofa with no pillows, no blankets, no sign of anyone having slept in it. Where was Frank? Had he seen him there sleeping before he crashed in his own bed?

CHAPTER THIRTY-THREE

Addison checked both of the bathrooms. "Frank?" he called out.

William stirred. "What are you doing?" he asked groggily.

Addison stood in the doorway between the rooms. "Everybody wake up. Frank is gone."

His concern was met with muddled grunts. A pillow flew past his head and hit the wall.

"He was here last night," William said.

"He's not here now," Addison said. "What if something happened?"

Don grumbled and sat up. "He's probably outside," he said. "Let's get dressed and go look for him. I'm sure he hasn't gone far."

The boys split into two groups and searched for Frank. Addison, William and Brandon checked the area around the motel. As patrons entered and exited restaurants and small businesses, the boys asked if they had seen someone fitting Frank's description. No one had.

Don and Victor retraced their steps to and from the lake. They found the garbage can they'd stashed their bottles in. On the shore, they discovered charred remnants of the previous night's campfire nearly undisturbed. The two separated and agreed to meet back at the motel.

Victor returned to the liquor store where they had purchased a case of Budweiser and a fifth of Jack Daniels. The acne-scarred, 20-something clerk barely looked up from the magazine he was thumbing through. Victor revisited the corner market where they had purchased two packages of hot dogs, two bags of potato chips and a box of Hostess Ding Dongs. No one remembered seeing Frank there the night before or that morning.

Don walked back to the lake again and combed the shore. Since he was a little boy, he'd heard stories about Lake Superior from his grandfather who had fished there in the summertime. It was so deep—over 1,200 feet in some areas—and so cold all year long that people who died in the lake stayed in the lake. Legend had it there were hundreds of bodies covering the bottom of Lake Superior that had been lost in shipwrecks and drownings.

There was no sign of Frank on the shoreline. It was a clear, sunny day and Don could see for miles. He paused to look out at the immense frozen lake before him. He hollered "FRAAANK!" into the wind. For the first time since he woke that morning, he began to worry about his friend.

Spotty details from the drunken night before resurfaced. He recalled arguing with Frank, horsing around, chucking his boot onto the lake. Of all the boys who comprised the Cretin Six, Don and Frank argued the most. Still, they were like brothers, and they loved each other like family.

Don walked back along the shore to the spot where the bonfire had been and peered out at the lake. He saw nothing but a vast expanse of white, a thick crust of snow covering the frozen water, and beyond it, cerulean blue sky. He stepped onto the ice, scanned the surface and walked farther out to where he was sure he'd tossed the boot. Nothing. He continued to walk and search, but he found no boot. And then, just a few yards ahead, he spotted open water. Where the jagged edge of the ice met the rippling dark liquid, there was a lump of something small and brown. It was one of Frank's wool-lined leather mittens.

"**D**id you find anything?" the boys asked Don when they met back at the motel.

"No sign of Frank at the beach," Don said, breathing heavily. The lie came so quickly, he wasn't entirely sure he'd said it.

"I think we better call the police," Addison said.

"Before we do," Don said, "we need to agree on our story."

"Story? We need to tell the truth," Addison said. "This is serious, man. One of the Cretin Six is missing."

"I'm not saying we should lie. I just think there are some details that would be best left out."

"Like what?" William asked.

"I don't think we should tell them Frank was drunk."

"We were all drunk."

"Let's say that we convinced someone outside the liquor store to buy us a six-pack to celebrate winning our division. Then we went to the shore to watch the Northern Lights, we made a fire, ate some food and each had one beer. I think we should leave it at that."

"That's lying," Addison said.

"There's a lot on the line. Frank could lose his spot on

Princeton's hockey team. Addison and Brandon, think about your scholarships. We all have a lot to lose," Don said.

* * *

"Hello, sir," Addison said, gripping the beige motel phone with his left hand and nervously picking at the corner of the Bible on the bedside table with his right. "My name is Addison McGuinn, and I'm calling from the Lake View Motel to report a missing person."

Within five minutes, a squad car and two policemen—one at least 6-foot-5-inches tall and thin, the other much shorter and portly—arrived at the motel. The police did a quick sweep of the two rooms and spoke with the boys collectively. The five of them stuck to their story: They arrived yesterday morning and played hockey with Duluth legend Tommy Wilson, which was arranged by Frank's father. Later that evening, they had a bonfire on the shore of Lake Superior. Sometime after midnight, they headed to their rooms at the Lake View Motel, which were booked by Frank's mother. Their original plan for today was to check out of the motel, grab breakfast at a local greasy spoon, and head back to the Twin Cities in the McGuinn family's Ford Fairlane.

"When I woke up this morning, I noticed Frank was gone," Addison said.

"Were you boys drinking alcohol or doing any drugs last night?" the tall officer asked, adjusting the visor on his cap as he looked down at the boys.

They all hesitated except Don. "We each had one beer," he said, feigning honor. "I'm the only one who thought we should say so."

"Why's that?" the stout officer asked. He glanced from boy to boy, examining their peaked faces. Addison swallowed and looked down at the matted green, gold and brown shag carpeting.

"We're the starting lineup for the Cretin High School hockey team, and we've got a championship game next week," Don said. "They were afraid we'd get in trouble for drinking, but I said we should be honest."

"You made it to the championships, huh? Good job, fellas," the officer replied.

"It's always best to tell the truth," the tall officer interjected.

"There's certainly no harm in one beer, son," his partner said, gripping Don's shoulder.

"That's what I told them," Don said, stuffing his hands into the front pockets of his jeans.

The officers contacted Frank's parents, who headed to Duluth immediately. The other boys' parents were notified as well. A second squad car arrived with two more officers. They spoke to the motel clerk who'd been on duty since 6 a.m. The attendant on duty before him during the overnight shift hadn't reported any issues, nor had any of the guests. The police knocked on the doors of several patrons and confirmed this. They searched the station wagon the twins had driven to Duluth in shifts the morning before—Brandon to a gas station in Hinkley, the halfway point, and Addison the remainder of the way. Aside from a mess of soda cans and candy wrappers littering the seats and floor, there were no clues in the vehicle as to Frank's whereabouts.

The four policemen conferred in the parking lot for 30 minutes and eventually invited the boys outside to join them. They stood on the strip of sidewalk that lined the entrances to the rooms.

"All right boys, we've got several officers out patrolling the area for your friend," the tall officer said. "In the meantime, we're going to need you to grab your stuff and follow us back to police headquarters. We'll get an official statement from each of you there."

"A statement?" Victor asked.

"We'll sit down with you individually and you'll tell us everything you can recall over the last 24 hours that might help us find your friend."

"What about Frank's stuff?" Addison asked.

"We'll collect his things," the tall officer said. "Once we have your statements, you can head home. I'm sure your parents will be glad to see you."

The boys did as they were told and barely uttered a word to one another as they followed the squad car to the station.

"Why did you say that?" Addison finally said to Don.

"We agreed to say we had one beer each," Don said defensively.

"I mean the part about you being the only one who thought we should admit we were drinking," Addison said. "That wasn't the truth."

CHAPTER THIRTY-FOUR

"Guys, this is serious," William interrupted. "Frank is missing."

"He's right," Brandon added. "Now more than ever, we need to be a team."

"Nice to meet you, Dr. Kopet," Maddie said. The therapist was younger than she thought she'd be, with long brown hair, warm brown eyes and flawless ivory skin.

"Please, call me Samantha," she said, adjusting the window blinds. "Take a seat wherever you feel most comfortable."

Light filtered through three large south-facing windows on one wall of the second-floor office. The adjacent wall was lined with floor-to-ceiling shelves filled with hundreds of books, plus a half-dozen succulent plants in ceramic pots, and several photographs in frames.

"You mentioned on the phone you'd done some research," Samantha said.

"Yes," Maddie said, sitting on the leather sofa, "to learn more about hypnotherapy."

Samantha sat in one of the green upholstered armchairs directly across from Maddie. Between the women was a coffee table with a stack of books and a box of tissues. "Have you read about the memory wars?"

"No," Maddie replied. She tucked a large throw pillow behind her on the sofa.

"Sigmund Freud developed theories about the subconscious, particularly regarding childhood trauma and repressed memories. As a result, he began using hypnosis to address the parts of his patients' subconscious that were causing unwanted thoughts, feelings or behaviors," Samantha explained. "There are researchers who don't believe it's possible to repress memories. They think some people avoid memories because facing them might have a negative impact on their life. This debate—about whether repressed memories are real or not—has been going on for decades. It's referred to as the memory wars."

"You believe they're real," Maddie confirmed.

"Absolutely," Samantha said.

"I mentioned that Hazel Bennett had referred me," Maddie said. "She said you were able to help her recover repressed memories from childhood. How would that work for someone like me who experienced TGA?"

Samantha took a sip of tea and placed the mug back on the table next to her. "Repressed memories can be the result of a challenging experience that is difficult for the mind to process. It can happen at any age, not just in childhood. Based on what you shared with me, you experienced a trauma. You may have seen something your brain is having trouble processing. Most people who experience transient global amnesia never recover memories during the hours leading up to it. Because you've had recurring nightmares about it, and some of the details were proven to be true, I think hypnosis could help you uncover more memories."

"I'll be honest," Maddie said, reaching for another pillow

and hugging it against her chest. "Knowing what really happened that night scares the shit out of me."

Samantha uncrossed her legs, scooted to the edge of her seat and looked Maddie straight in the eye. "I understand," she said. "I am often asked why someone would want to recover memories that were painful or traumatic."

"What do you say?" Maddie asked, tears pricking at the corners of her eyes. She reached for a tissue.

"I believe anxiety, phobias and other conditions can be the result of repressed memories. As someone who specializes in recovered memory therapy, I help people better understand the origins of their mental health challenges so they can deal with them. For example, during the course of therapy, a patient may recover a traumatic memory of child abuse. By discussing this memory, they may better understand the feelings and relationships they experience as an adult."

Maddie thought about Hazel and wondered what exactly she had endured during her childhood. She admired the young woman for her bravery in addressing her issues. She was inspired to do the same.

"OK," Maddie said. "Let's give it a try."

* * *

"Well? How was it?" Simone asked, the second Maddie entered the office. "I've been trying to reach you, but your phone is going straight to voicemail."

"My phone is dead and the charger I keep in my car has

disappeared," Maddie said. She set her briefcase on a chair and hung up her coat. "The therapist was wonderful. But we weren't able to access any of my repressed memories during the session."

"I'm sorry," Simone said. "I know you had high hopes."

"We're going to try again," Maddie said, digging the phone out of her bag. "I scheduled a second appointment for next week."

"I'll trade you," Simone said. She took Maddie's cell phone and handed her a sheet of paper from the printer. "Here's the other reason I was trying to reach you." Simone plugged Maddie's phone into the charger on her desk.

"Authorities search for missing Apple Valley man," Maddie read aloud from a Star Tribune news article from 2002. She continued reading:

"Choice Car Service owner Ralph Finney reported an employee, Mohamed Assad, missing to the Minneapolis police on Sunday when the driver failed to return the vehicle. Finney became concerned after he had not heard from Assad and requested a welfare check at his Apple Valley townhome. Apple Valley police found no one present at the address.

"According to Finney, Choice Car Service had recently added a fleet of luxury cars; Assad was driving a black 2002 BMW 540i Sedan. Assad is believed to be in his early 60s, approximately 5-feet-8-inches tall, with a slender build, graying hair and brown eyes.

"Assad began working for Choice Car Service in 1990, one year after he immigrated to the United States from Canada. According to Finney, Assad is a model employee. 'This is very unusual and completely unlike the Mohamed Assad I know. He is always prompt, a loyal friend, and a respected member of the Choice Car Service family. I am at a loss to understand how a car and its driver can literally vanish. We are praying the authorities will locate Mohamed and bring him back safely.'"

"Is this someone I should know?" Maddie asked, squinting at the fuzzy photo of the missing man.

"The skull you found," Simone said slowly, "was identified as Mohamed Assad. The man in the article."

Maddie sucked in a breath and held it in her lungs. She felt light-headed. She'd known all along the remains were a human's, but the reality of those bones belonging to a real person with family and friends hit her like a ton of bricks. She lowered herself into one of the lobby chairs.

Simone went to the kitchen and filled a glass of water. "I know it's a lot to process," she said, handing Maddie the glass.

"He was someone's loved one," Maddie said, taking a sip. "He has been missing for more than a decade and those people have gotten no answers. They've had no closure."

"The case has been reopened," Simone said. She rubbed Maddie's shoulder gently. "They might just get the answers they deserve."

* * *

"You doing OK?" Simone asked, poking her head into Maddie's office.

"I'm fine," she said. "With this caseload, there isn't much

time to think about anything else." Maddie patted a pile of folders stacked several inches high on the corner of her desk. "Did I tell you I asked our landlord about the vacant suite next door?"

"That's wonderful, Maddie," Simone said. "Is the space bigger than ours?"

"It's a mirror image of our space. We could literally cut a hole in the wall and double our footprint."

"That would be fabulous," Simone said. "We'd have more room for files, and we could add support staff."

"And my new law partner would have a proper office," Maddie said with a wink. "I have an idea about support staff."

"I'm all ears," Simone said.

"You know I met with Hazel Bennett a couple of times. I think I mentioned she completed an internship at Best Buy, decided corporate law was not for her, and wants to specialize in family law." Simone nodded. "She was recently offered an internship at Metro Family Law but turned it down."

"She did?" Simone asked. "They're one of the best in town."

"She was concerned about the firm's lack of diversity."

"It's definitely an old boys' club," Simone said.

"What do you think about offering her a part-time position here?" Maddie asked. "She's whip-smart, she knows exactly what she wants, and she's not afraid to go after it."

"Sounds a lot like you at her age," Simone said. She took a moment to consider the idea. "I'd love to meet her," she said. "I'll set up an interview."

As Simone entered the quaint cafe, she immediately recognized Ralph Finney, the owner of Choice Car Service, from the company's website. On the site, he was pictured standing with several employees in front of a fleet of shiny black luxury vehicles. His hair was dark and neatly trimmed, his handlebar mustache was graying. He was handsome in the photo and even more dashing in person.

Simone had reached out to Ralph through a web contact form. She addressed him directly, introduced herself, mentioned the law firm and asked if he might be willing to meet. He called her cell phone the same day. Though many years had passed since Mohamed Assad had gone missing, and news about the discovery of his remains had been devastating, Ralph was willing to discuss his friend and co-worker. He suggested they get together at a cafe in St. Paul.

As their eyes met, Simone waved. Ralph nodded in acknowledgment and raised his hand.

"I'm going to order a coffee—would you like anything?" Simone asked.

"No thanks, I'm on my third cup," Ralph confessed with a sly grin. "I have to limit myself or I'll be wide awake at midnight."

"I'm the same way," Simone said, returning the smile.

She ordered a coffee at the counter and read the specials on the chalkboard while she waited. If she hadn't already eaten, the quiche would have been tempting.

When Simone approached the table with her drink, Ralph rose and shook her hand. She unwrapped herself from her coat, took a seat, told him a bit more about the firm and how it was Maddie who'd originally found Mohamed's skull. She clarified that the firm was not involved in the newly reopened criminal case; she was looking into it on her own.

"Given the circumstances, Ms. Cummins feels a connection to Mr. Assad. She's been having dreams about him calling out to her."

"Mohamed deserves justice," Ralph said with a lump in his throat. "He lost his life needlessly. The authorities couldn't seem to get past their biases about Mohamed and never seemed committed to finding the killer."

"That's exactly why I feel compelled to help," Simone said. "Is it all right if I take notes?"

"Of course," he said. "They made me so angry."

Simone clicked her pen. "The authorities?"

"Yes," he said. "One of their theories was that Mohamed fled the country on his own accord. Took the car and drove back to Canada. They speculated it had something to do with a family member in Iran who had ties to the Islamic Revolution."

"You didn't believe it?" Simone asked.

"Not for a minute," Ralph said. "Mohamed earned a degree in mathematics. His wife, Minoo, studied to be a physician. When Khomeini came to power in the '70s, the two of them fled the country with just the clothes on their backs." He explained that the Assads spent over a decade living in British Columbia, where they worked and started a family. After several months of treatment, Minoo died of cancer. "Mohamed came to the United States for a fresh start. He made a wonderful life for his three children. They went on to graduate from prestigious universities." Ralph shook his head. "It made no sense that he would abandon his family and a life he was so proud of."

Simone processed the unfolding details of the case. She tapped her lacquered purple nails rhythmically on the tabletop. She found investigative work invigorating, especially when it involved seeking justice for people of color. Thoughts of becoming an attorney had played like a soft melody in the nooks of her mind for years. Now the music was reaching a crescendo. There was no valid reason not to take her career to the next level. She wanted to be a facilitator of change. She would talk to her daughters about her plans to take the bar exam when they were together on Thanksgiving.

"What do you know about Mr. Assad's last passenger?" Simone asked.

"Trey Calvers was a regular customer," Ralph said. Simone wrote the name at the top of the legal pad and circled it. "He always requested Mohamed as his driver. He was questioned by the police, but after they theorized one of Mohamed's family members had something to do with it, that became their main focus."

"What do you recall about Mr. Calvers?" Simone asked.

"Mohamed drove him to casinos throughout Minnesota— Mystic Lake, Grand Portage, Treasure Island. Trey was a big gambler. He treated Mohamed well. Always paid in cash and was a hefty tipper."

"Did you contact Mr. Calvers when you couldn't reach Mohamed?"

"I called him as soon as it was apparent Mohamed hadn't returned the car," Ralph said. "He confirmed Mohamed had dropped him off at home. We never spoke again." Ralph's voice cracked.

"I'm very sorry, Mr. Finney," Simone said. She set down her pen and patted his arm.

"What happened to Mohamed has weighed on me for years. Choice Car Service is a small family-owned business, and employees are like kin. I would have hired a PI if I'd had the means to do so."

* * *

When Simone arrived at the office, contractors had already demolished part of the wall to the connecting suite. Seeing the expansion of the space was the final push she needed. She would take the next step in her career and register for the bar exam in February.

Despite the sheet of murky plastic that hung between the

spaces, thick drywall dust coated every surface. The furnishings were wrapped in moving blankets and had been temporarily pushed out of the way. New furniture for Simone's office had been ordered, and just a few remaining items needed to be removed from her old desk. She tossed the legal pad with her notes from the conversation with Ralph into a box. She removed the hanging files from both lower desk drawers and put those in the box as well.

"Good morning!" Maddie said, beaming as she entered. "It's happening! The firm is growing!"

"What's the saying—it's always darkest before the dawn?" Simone laughed. "The space will be wonderful when it's done, but right now it's chaos." She smoothed a strip of packing tape across the gap and sealed the box.

"Thanks for your flexibility and agreeing to work from home for a few days," Maddie said. "I think it's the best option."

"It's only temporary," Simone said, as she wrote "desk files" in black marker on the side of the carton. "I don't think either of us anticipated the space would be completely unusable during construction."

"I just need to grab my current files," Maddie said. "What can I help pack?"

"This is it," Simone said. She tucked the box she'd just taped under the desk and gathered her purse.

As they left the office together, Simone didn't mention her meeting with Ralph Finney. The information Ralph provided was certainly revealing, but she wanted to research Mohamed's disappearance further before filling Maddie in.

"Remember your first business suite?" Simone asked. "The entire space was smaller than your current office."

"We've come a long way," Maddie said. "Our new space will be so expansive that we may never see each other."

* * *

Later in the week, with renovations at the office moving full speed ahead, Maddie and Simone planned an early afternoon meeting with Hazel at the coffee shop down the street. It was quiet there then, and the perfect place to discuss the law clerk position they thought might be of interest to Hazel while she completed her final year of law school.

Hazel was already at the coffee shop when Maddie and Simone arrived. Her hair was smoothed into a sleek low ponytail. She wore an animal print blouse with a pewter-colored leather jacket, a mid-length black skirt and ankle boots. She wasn't conservatively attired the way law students were advised to dress for job interviews, but Maddie admired Hazel's pluck. She seemed to bring her true self to every meeting. Maddie introduced Hazel to Simone and, beverages in hand, they settled in near the stone fireplace to chat.

Maddie presented the job description and summarized the firm's needs. "Simone and I would like someone to join our team who can prepare legal documents and research, analyze and compile case materials. It's a behind-the-scenes position. Does that appeal to you?"

"Conducting research, reviewing documents, organizing information—it's all crucial for planning for court, and these are areas where I excel," Hazel said. "Family law speaks to me in ways other areas of specialty have not. I'm hoping to secure a position where I can use my strengths and provide support to families experiencing difficult situations. The hands-on knowledge I'd gain at Cummins Law Office would give me a solid foundation for my career as a family law attorney. I'm especially passionate about working for a women-owned and led firm."

Maddie smiled and turned toward Simone, who asked the next question. "Expanding the firm is a priority. I will be sitting for the bar in February, so we'll be down a staff member for about six weeks while I prepare. We plan to add a contract paralegal. Would you be comfortable taking on extra responsibility while you are still in school?"

"Absolutely!" Hazel said. "The added experience would be a bonus! I graduate next May and plan to take the bar in July. Perhaps I'd even learn something from your experience going through the process."

"I hope to add a third attorney at some point in the future." Maddie said. "That means there would be potential for you to grow within the firm—if it's a fit." She looked over at Simone who nodded. "For now, we'd love to have you join us as a clerk."

"I'd be honored to work with both of you!" Hazel said.

"When can you start?" Simone asked.

"I can start right away and work around my class schedule."

Hazel said enthusiastically. "After finals, I could work full-time in December and over Christmas break."

"Congratulations and welcome to Cummins Law Office!" Maddie said.

M addie closed her laptop. She gathered the legal pad she'd been using for notes and the file folders for the cases she was working on and stacked them on top of the computer with her eyeglasses. She pushed it all out of the way, to the center of the kitchen island, and pulled her dinner plate and glass of wine closer. It had been a long day, and she was working much later than she would have had she been in the office. It was one of the biggest challenges of working from home—getting completely absorbed in casework and losing track of time.

The half-eaten broiled chicken breast and roasted vegetables on her plate had gone cold, and the white wine in her glass was room temperature. She stood to bring her dishes to the sink, and her phone pinged. It was a text from Paula in their group chat with Constance, a link to the Minnesota Public Radio news website. She froze when she read the headline: "Prominent Minnesota businessman Addison McGuinn has died." She scrolled down to the article:

"This afternoon, a representative from the St. Louis County sheriff's office informed Minnesota Public Radio that the county medical examiner confirmed a body discovered yesterday was that of prominent Minnesota businessman Addison McGuinn. According to the representative, yesterday morning officers were called to the Indian Lake Campground by the St. Louis County Department of Natural Resources. Officers found McGuinn's car in the parking lot and discovered his body with a gunshot wound in a wooded area 300 feet from the vehicle. Evidence at the scene indicated the wound was self-inflicted. McGuinn was transported by helicopter to St. Luke's Hospital, a level one trauma center in Duluth, where he was pronounced dead.

"Addison McGuinn was the twin brother of Brandon McGuinn, with whom he founded Commonwealth Banc. The McGuinn brothers were recently sued by the trustee in Minnesota auto dealer Don Koch's bankruptcy case. The suit alleged that Addison and Brandon McGuinn colluded with Koch to hide assets. The McGuinn brothers denied any wrongdoing and filed a counter suit to have the charges dismissed."

"WTF?" Maddie responded in the text chain to Paula and Constance.

"Breakfast tomorrow?" Paula responded.

"I'll be there."

* * *

Maddie was 30 minutes late arriving to the diner. "So sorry," she said as she joined Paula and Constance at their usual table. "I hope you got my text and ordered without me."

"Is everything OK?" Paula asked, noticing the dark bags under her best friend's eyes.

Maddie unbuttoned her coat and slid into the booth next to Constance. "I'm not sleeping," she said with a sigh. "My recurring nightmares are back with a vengeance."

Paula filled the empty mug near Maddie with coffee. "I wish there was something I could do to help," she said.

"I have a second appointment with the therapist today," Maddie said.

Bonnie appeared with plates of steaming food and placed them in front of Constance and Paula. "Morning, Maddie. Can I get you something other than coffee?" she asked.

"Good morning, Bonnie. I'd like a blueberry scone, please."

"Coming right up," Bonnie said.

"How was your first appointment with the therapist?" Constance asked, shaking salt and pepper on her eggs.

"We weren't able to recover any memories, so we're going to give it one more shot," Maddie said. "My mind has been spinning since the skull was identified. Now my dreams are haunted by an actual person—Mohamed Assad—and he is begging me to help."

"You know the case has been reopened, right?" Constance said.

Maddie nodded as she took a bite of her scone.

"Do you think you witnessed something that could be helpful in solving the crime?"

"I have no idea," Maddie said. "According to Samantha, it's possible I saw something my brain is having trouble processing. Hypnosis could reveal what happened prior to the TGA, during those hours when I was stumbling through fields and tripping over human remains."

Paula shook her head and a deep crease appeared between her brows.

"I know that look," Maddie said. "What's your concern?"

"I'm not convinced knowing what happened that night would make things better," Paula said. "Perhaps it's best to leave well enough alone."

"Leave well enough alone?" Maddie asked, miffed. "Have you forgotten you're the one who you encouraged me to write down my nightmares in the first place?"

"I haven't forgotten," Paula said. "But what happens if you recall specific events, and it traumatizes you all over again?"

"Then I can finally process the whole ordeal and move on with my life."

"Fine," Paula said. "Don't forget that both the ER physician and your primary care doctor said most people who experience TGA don't recover their memories. There's a good chance you'll never know what happened. Then what?"

Bonnie appeared at the table, her squeaking shoe breaking the tension. "How is everything?" she asked.

"Everything's great," Constance said, forcing a smile.

The waitress moved on to the next booth.

"Let's talk about something else," Maddie said.

"Yes," Constance said, unlocking her phone. "Have you seen this?"

Maddie took the phone and scrolled through the news article on the screen. It was another story about Addison McGuinn. "I haven't seen this one," she said. "It looks like a repeat of the article from yesterday."

"There were a half dozen more just like it this morning, and not a single one of them mentions the long-term relationship between the McGuinn brothers and Don Koch," Paula said.

Maddie took a moment to digest the information. "There's a bigger story than the one the media is focusing on."

"Yup," Paula said. "Because no one has uncovered it yet."

"Don's diabolical behavior started when he was a teenager. He is connected to multiple deaths over the past four decades. There's much more to it than business dealings gone bad."

"Exactly," Paula said.

Simone's daughters were on her mind as she opened the oven, checked the browning bird and reflected on the past year. In addition to regular updates about their busy lives, conversations with her daughters often included talk of Don Koch as they brought up news stories they'd seen or read. With the latest reports about Addison McGuinn and the McGuinn brothers' connections to Don, Simone considered where the Thanksgiving table talk might go. As she whisked fine flour into broth for savory gravy, she made up her mind: They would not discuss one word of it today.

Thanksgiving was Simone's favorite holiday. Perhaps because it has been her late husband Edward's as well. His death from colon cancer at age 40 had devastated her. A week before he died, their close-knit family celebrated Thanksgiving together, and it was one of Simone's most cherished memories.

After Edward passed, her grief was overwhelming. At first, Simone was angry with him for dying and leaving her to raise their three young children. There was so much uncertainty about how they would survive. Simone quickly realized the bitterness could tear off pieces of her until there was nothing but a shell.

She was not going to let that happen. When her own mother came to her in her dreams, Simone recalled the grace, strength and resiliency the woman had possessed, and began to sense her guiding presence.

It had not been easy to be a single working mother. Maya, Sasha and Arianna pitched in, taking after-school jobs, excelling academically, obtaining well-earned scholarships for college. Simone flipped through the memories like pages in a scrapbook. A smile crossed her lips.

Fragrant aromas drifted through the house—turkey, stuffing and corn casserole baked in the oven. Potatoes boiled on the stove, soon to be mashed to perfection. Everyone was responsible for a specific dish: Maddie was preparing her homemade cranberry sauce; Paula was making a green bean casserole; Maya was responsible for cornbread and collard greens; Sasha was overseeing salads and the sweet potato pie. Arianna, who had just flown in from California, had brought several bottles of Napa Valley wine with her.

Simone was anxious for everyone to arrive. Dinner was at 5 p.m. and the kitchen clock displayed 4:04. Minutes later, the sisters arrived together, arms laden with food. Arianna's television acting schedule often kept her away longer than her mother and siblings would like, and they were thrilled she'd made it home. There was lively chatter as the four women gathered around the large granite-topped kitchen island.

"I love seeing your face on my TV every week." Sasha opened the overstuffed refrigerator and deftly reorganized containers to make room for her salads. "It's like we're together, even when we're not."

"What's Corrine Davis really like to work with?" Maya chimed in.

"I learn something from her every day," Arianna said. "She's the kind of actress I aspire to be."

"You're an amazing actress in your own right," Sasha said.

"We're so proud of you," Maya said.

"Acting doesn't compare to bringing babies into the world and slaying computer hackers," Arianna said.

"I'm proud of all my girls," Simone said, her face radiant. "Before Maddie and Paula arrive, there's something I need to discuss with you."

"This sounds serious, Mama," Maya said, her brow furrowed.

"It is," Simone acknowledged. "In a good way."

"What is it?" Arianna asked. She wrapped her thick cardigan around her slender frame.

Simone wiped her hands on a dish towel and took a seat at the kitchen island. "Maddie asked me to sit for the bar and become a partner—"

Before she could finish the sentence, joyous shouts reverberated through the house.

"We wondered if we would ever hear you say those words!" Sasha threw her arms around her mother's neck. "You're an amazing paralegal, but attorney at law is your true calling."

"Amen to that," Maya agreed. "For years the three of us have talked about how you should be practicing law. We didn't want to push the topic. We knew you would make the decision when you were ready."

"When is the bar exam?" Arianna asked.

"At the end of February." Simone took in the smiles on her daughters' faces. "I will take time off work to study and enroll in a refresher course. Maddie and I will find a paralegal to cover me, and in the meantime, we've hired on a third-year legal student as a law clerk."

The doorbell rang, and Sasha hurried to answer it. It was Maddie and Paula, who had carpooled to Simone's house. As they entered, Sasha was unable to contain her excitement. "Mama is taking the bar!"

Within minutes, flutes of champagne were raised to toast the momentous occasion. Amid the happy talk and catching up on everyone's lives, Simone expertly carved the succulent turkey and arranged it on a platter. The others placed the serving bowls of side dishes on the table.

"Calories do not count today!" Simone announced as they dug into the feast.

While they ate, Sasha was the first to ask about the Koch case. "What's going on with his criminal trial?"

"I'd like to keep the conversation focused on what we're thankful for," Simone said.

"You can't expect us not to talk about the biggest case of the year," Sasha said.

Paula swirled the wine in her glass and looked at Simone, who sighed and gave a small nod. "Don's case is going to trial," Paula said.

"What about Addison McGuinn?" Sasha pressed. "The media is making a connection between his death and his business dealings with Don Koch."

Paula set down her wine glass. "The McGuinn brothers' business has been under investigation for issuing fraudulent bank loans to and hiding assets for Don Koch. Some media outlets have made a presumption of Addison McGuinn's guilt based on his suicide, but it's not that simple."

"Addison McGuinn?" Maya asked as she made a connection she hadn't earlier. "That's Gail McGuinn's dad. Gail and I played intramural soccer together in 10th grade. They had a brand-new house at Bohn's Point on Lake Minnetonka."

"The girl who used to flip her hair when she talked?" Sasha asked.

"Yes," Maya said. "Mr. and Mrs. McGuinn had a party for us in their backyard the summer after our team took second place."

"That's right," Sasha said. "You borrowed my new swimsuit that day."

"Their place was beautiful, and the boathouse was an exact replica of the house," Maya said.

"Those boathouses on Lake Minnetonka are fancier than most people's houses," Arianna said. "Including some of the celebrity homes I've seen in California."

"Have you and Gail kept in touch?" Sasha asked.

"No, we haven't. I'm sorry she lost her dad. Her parents were so nice to all of us girls," Maya said and paused. "Mr. McGuinn took us out on their boat that day and anchored it in Crystal

Bay. It was so hot that we all decided to jump in and swim back to shore."

As soon as the words had left Maya's mouth, Paula and Maddie looked at each other. "You swam from the bay to shore?" Paula asked.

"Yes," Maya confirmed.

"Do you remember how long it took?" Paula asked.

Maya thought about it for a few seconds. "I'd say we were all back to the shore within 15 minutes."

* * *

After a delicious dinner, and several more hours of conversation, dessert and dishes, Paula was deep in thought as she drove Maddie home. She'd had meetings with Constance early in the investigation of Peter Dickrell's homicide. There had been a search of Addison McGuinn's residence that took place prior to his death. The FBI hadn't uncovered any evidence that connected him to Peter's death. Since Maya brought it up at dinner, Paula was distracted by a singular thought: In all of their conversations about the case, Constance never mentioned the McGuinns' boathouse.

"Paula?" Maddie said, when she realized her friend wasn't listening.

"Yes, sorry," she responded. "My mind is elsewhere."

"I know exactly what your mind is," Maddie said. "You're thinking about Peter Dickrell's homicide."

"You know me well," Paula said.

"You're thinking Don was probably on the boat with Peter the night he was killed." Maddie said, "and that he swam to the McGuinns' after everything went down."

"Do me a favor," Paula said, unlocking her phone and handing it to Maddie. "Text Constance and ask if the boathouse was searched."

* * *

Early Black Friday morning, as devoted shoppers formed long lines outside of big-box stores, hoping to be among the first to snag ridiculously low-priced electronics and holiday gifts, Constance filed an affidavit with the court for an emergency warrant.

Just a few hours later, the FBI searched the McGuinns' boathouse and discovered men's apparel—khaki pants, a white Ralph Lauren Polo shirt, brown leather Sperry Docksider shoes and white socks—that appeared to have been discarded months ago. It was clear the items had been wet when they were tucked inside a row of locker-like cabinets that held life vests and other boating equipment. They were bagged and immediately sent to the FBI's lab for forensic testing.

Maddie and Simone spent several hours over the weekend at the newly expanded and renovated offices, preparing for the reopening and Hazel's first day. They cleaned the construction dust and waste left behind by the crew. The movers delivered and arranged the new furnishings according to the architect's plans, and Maddie and Simone promptly rearranged them. They reconnected the Wi-Fi, computers, printers and phones, and tested the equipment to make sure everything was working. Maddie started to unpack the law library and place the books on the custom-built shelves. Simone got the sleek modern kitchen in order. After several hours of work, there was still more to do, but the place looked great, and they knew everything would come together in time.

On Monday, Maddie's excitement was impossible to contain. She stopped at the coffee shop down the street and ordered three lattes—hers with an extra shot of espresso—and a box of scones. As the elevator opened and Maddie stepped out, she smiled at the new entryway—a wall of glass with double doors in the center. A temporary sign to the left of the doors read "Cummins

Law Office," but the glass would soon be etched with the firm's new name, "Cummins and Backstrom."

Simone and Hazel chatted in the reception area. Both were dressed casually per Maddie's edict—Simone in leggings and a tunic, and Hazel in jeans and a turtleneck sweater. They noticed Maddie approach with a cardboard tray of coffee and a pastry box.

"Good morning!" Maddie said as she entered. "I brought treats in celebration of our new space and Hazel's first day."

Simone took the coffee and pastries and set them on the reception desk. "I'll get the napkins," she said as she jogged to the kitchen. "I know just where they are!"

"What a warm welcome," Hazel said, beaming. "I was just telling Simone how much I love the blue and gray color palette you selected. It's soothing and sophisticated."

"That's what we were going for," Maddie said. She handed each of the women a latte, grabbed her own drink, and asked excitedly, "Who wants to hear the game plan for today?"

Simone noticed the words "extra shot" marked on Maddie's cup. "How much espresso do you have in there?" she asked, laughing.

"I've been up since 4 a.m." Maddie wiped the foam off her lips. "More weird dreams."

"Have you had a session with Samantha?" Hazel asked. She removed the lid from her latte and took a cautious sip.

"I've had two hypnotherapy sessions with her, but no luck recovering any memories." Maddie said. "At this point, she says it's unlikely I'll remember anything."

CHAPTER THIRTY-NINE

"I'm sorry," Hazel said.

"It's OK, we knew it was a long shot," Maddie said.

"Something tells me once Mohamed Assad's killer has been found, your nightmares will cease," Simone said.

"You're probably right," Maddie said. She took a long drink of her latte. "Now, back to the game plan: Simone, I'd like you to decide where the artwork will go. Someone from building maintenance will be here shortly to hang the paintings. You'll need to show them where."

"Sounds great."

"Hazel, I'd like you to finish unpacking the legal boxes, which are filled with client files. Simone or I can show you how the file cabinets are currently organized. If you have ideas to make it better, we'd love your input."

"Perfect," Hazel said. "I'm an expert organizer."

"I'm going to finish unpacking the books and cataloging the law library," Maddie said.

* * *

Maddie, Simone and Hazel spent their morning getting the office in order. They took a midday break, put on their coats and gloves, and walked a few blocks to The Freight House. Perched along the edge of the scenic St. Croix River, the restaurant offered hearty fare—soups, chili, burgers and sandwiches—perfect for a cold December day. After lunch, they headed back to the office and assessed what was left to do. They had accomplished almost everything on the list. The artwork had been hung, the library was shipshape, most of the boxes had been emptied and broken down for recycling, and the client files had been sorted.

"I've got a couple more boxes to go through," Hazel said. "I'll be done in no time."

"Wonderful," Simone said. "Maddie, why don't we meet in your office and review case files?"

"Great idea," Maddie said. "It will be nice to finally talk about cases face to face."

Twenty minutes into their meeting, Simone and Maddie's conversation was interrupted by a loud gasp in the other room.

"Hazel? Are you OK?" Maddie asked.

She and Simone stood quickly and found Hazel sitting on the floor in the file room next to a box of miscellaneous office supplies. In her shaking hands was a yellow legal pad with notes in Simone's handwriting.

"Hazel, honey," Simone said, crouching next to her. "What's the matter?"

Hazel was momentarily mute.

Maddie took the notepad from her and inspected it. "What's this?" she asked, looking at Simone.

Simone glanced at the pad. "Notes from a meeting with Ralph Finney, Mohamed Assad's former employer," she said. "I reached out shortly after the skull was identified and mentioned I was unofficially investigating the case. We met for coffee. With everything going on, I'd forgotten all about it. This notepad must have gotten tossed in the box with the other things from my desk."

Maddie recognized the name Trey Calvers scrawled in

Simone's handwriting at the top of the pad. Hazel's mother had described him as one of Don's henchmen and said she wouldn't let him near her daughters. She didn't elaborate but now, based on Hazel's reaction, Maddie imagined the worst.

Maddie had never mentioned the details from her conversation with Lisa or the name Trey Calvers to Simone. "Did you and Ralph Finney discuss Trey Calvers?" she asked.

"Yes," Simone said. "He was Mohamed Assad's last client, before Mr. Assad and the BMW he was driving went missing."

"Simone—" Maddie felt her heart thump quickly against her ribcage. "Trey Calvers used to work for—" She paused as she began to connect the dots in her mind.

"Don Koch," Hazel said.

JULY 1993

It was the third warmest day of the summer—nearly 100 degrees—and the National Weather Service had issued an excessive heat warning for all of central and southern Minnesota. Experts recommended staying indoors, in air-conditioned buildings, and advised limiting outdoor activity to the morning hours or later in the evening. After an early picnic of peanut butter and jelly sandwiches, followed by playing with dolls in the shade, Lisa Bennett carried her red-cheeked 4-year-old, Anna, inside for a nap. Hazel, who was 6 at the time, and adamantly opposed to naps, continued to play in the lush backyard landscape of the Koch family's stately Minnetonka home.

For a while, she jumped and danced in the grass through the sprinkler's swinging arches of cool water. Without her little sister, she grew bored and went back to playing with her Barbie doll-sized pink and purple plastic RV. The slide out extended from the side to reveal the camper's interior, which featured a miniature kitchen with a stove and refrigerator and sleeping quarters with a cozy bed. Hazel imagined her family taking a trip in an RV just like it.

As she pretended Ken was making pancakes for Barbie for breakfast, the sun dried her wispy blonde hair, and the intense heat began to warm her scalp. If her mother had been outside, she would have insisted Hazel put on her pink baseball cap and sit under the sugar maple. Hazel had a better idea. She stuffed her dolls inside the camper and carried them to one of her favorite places to hide and play—below the backyard deck. It was cooler there, the soil slightly damp beneath her bare feet, and it wasn't too dark; flashes of sunshine danced past the day lilies in the surrounding gardens and through the wooden lattice that encased the deck's underside.

As she set up camp for her dolls, Hazel was startled by the sound of her father. "Trey's a fucking DEAD MAN," she heard him say. He was not speaking loudly, but he was using his angry voice, the one Hazel didn't like.

She knew Trey was a man who worked with her father, and he had said they were friends. She didn't know Trey as well as his other friends, the ones who insisted she call them "uncle"— Uncle Addison, Uncle Brandon, Uncle Victor, Uncle William. And she didn't hug him like her father insisted she do when she greeted those men. She remembered meeting Trey, and how her father made her shake his hand. Was he angry with his friend? Had he done something wrong at work? She couldn't remember what his job was—did he sell cars? Had Trey died? Weren't people usually sad when someone died?

"Do you understand me?" Don growled through clenched teeth.

Now Hazel was certain he was mad and not sad. He'd used those same words with her once, sounded just like that as he grabbed her face and squeezed her jaw and told her she wasn't allowed to go into his home office, and she was never, ever to rummage through his desk drawers. She had only been looking for a pencil and paper. She had wanted to write her father a note.

"I understand, boss," Hazel heard a man who was not her father say. She didn't recognize his voice.

She looked up between the small gaps in the deck boards, hoping to get a glimpse of who it was. She saw only their feet. She willed herself to sit still like a statue. Whenever her father talked about his work, he made her leave the room. He said business conversations were for adults only. If he knew she was eavesdropping, she would be in big trouble.

Despite the sweltering heat, Hazel began to shiver. She hugged her skinny knees to her chest and listened as her father and the man talked about money and casinos and gambling and how Trey had a problem.

"He's demanding a hundred grand, and threatening to go to the police about Philip Lane," Don said. "No one threatens me. It's fucking extortion. He's a dead man."

What had her father meant when he said Trey was a dead man?

Last Halloween, Hazel's best friend Jada's big brother wore a mask with a burned and disfigured face and tufts of hair and gloves with knives for fingers. He told the girls the story of Freddy Krueger, a child killer who'd been set on fire by the parents of one of his victims and came back from the dead to haunt their dreams and murder them.

"That's just a movie," Hazel had said unaffectedly to the boy, though Jada was terrified. When Hazel told her mother, Lisa confirmed that Freddy was a make-believe character; he wasn't real. When someone died, she assured her, they could not come back to life. Maybe her mother was wrong.

Hazel listened as Don walked back and forth on the boards above her. He was making plans with the man whose voice she didn't know.

She held her knees tighter, tried to stop her body from shaking. Why did she feel so cold when it was so warm outside? She wished she'd thought of bringing the towel she'd used to dry off after running through the sprinkler; she could cover up with it, get warm again. Her stomach began to flip the way it had when she'd come down with the flu the previous winter. Her mother had given her Sprite and crackers then. Maybe that's what she needed now.

The top of her head began to tingle. Her heart thumped so loudly that she could hear it pounding in her ears. The sound of her heart muffled the voices of her father and the man. She heard what they said intermittently now: kill, bastard, bullet, head, bury, farm.

Sweat dripped from Hazel's forehead into her eyes. She blinked hard and something on the ground caught her eye. A small brown and white garter snake slithered along the edge of the lattice. Hazel threw up her lunch, and everything went dark.

* * *

"No! No! No!"

"I'm here, sweetie!" Lisa ran into her daughter's bedroom and wrapped the child in her arms. "Mommy's right here. It was just a bad dream."

It was the third night in a row that Hazel had cried out in her sleep. And the third night she had insisted, as Lisa tucked her into bed, that the light be left on in the Jack-and-Jill bathroom between her bedroom and her sister Anna's. Hazel had always been a courageous girl, and she had never been afraid of the dark. She hadn't been herself since suffering from what Lisa thought had been heat stroke. Lisa chastised herself for not insisting Hazel come inside sooner. The recurring nightmares were starting to concern her.

"He was chasing me," Hazel said with a whimper.

"It was just a bad dream," Lisa said, brushing Hazel's wet mop of hair out of her eyes and kissing her on the forehead. "Dreams aren't real."

"He is real!" Hazel cried. She wanted to tell her mother it was Trey, the man her father worked with, who was chasing her.

"Hazel," Lisa turned to face her daughter and looked directly into her wide eyes. "What makes you think the man in your bad dreams is real?" she asked.

"Because—" Hazel said and hesitated.

"It's OK," Lisa said. "You can tell me."

Hazel buried her face into her mother's chest and sobbed.

"Honey, please," Lisa pleaded, "tell Mommy what's wrong."

Hazel's sobs grew louder, and her small body quivered. Her skin was sticky with sweat and tears. She could not be consoled.

Hazel took a drink of water and set down the glass. The blush had returned to her cheeks.

Simone, who sat beside Hazel at the conference table, put an arm around her shoulder. "I'm so sorry you endured that as a child," she said. "I understand why you locked up those memories and threw away the key."

"Are you sure you want to continue?" Maddie asked.

"Yes," Hazel said. "I buried the memories more than 20 years ago. Thanks to Samantha, I now recall what happened. I can actually talk about it. I can finally work through the trauma."

"Take your time, hon," Simone said. "One thing Maddie's episode of TGA has taught us is that revisiting a trauma can be just as horrifying as the original event." She looked across the table at Maddie, who nodded.

Hazel may have been comfortable sharing the information, but Maddie wasn't sure she was ready to hear it. Trey Calvers was a long-ago Koch Automotive Group employee who issued Don an ultimatum. Where was he now? Was he dead? He was Mohamed Assad's last client before he went missing, and Mohamed was dead. Philip Lane was the Duluth general contractor who confronted Don about not getting paid. He wound up dead. Peter Dickrell agreed to testify at his former son-in-law's criminal trial. He was dead.

"Hazel, I have some friends I'd like you to talk to," Maddie said. "Constance Lopez is a federal agent and Paula Milton is a U.S. attorney. They are working on Don's criminal case. You have information that could help prove his involvement in a homicide—perhaps more than one. Would it be all right if I called them?"

"I don't—" Hazel said and paused. She stared at the water that remained in her glass and said nothing.

Several minutes passed and Simone patted Hazel's arm. "You've had one hell of a first day on the job," she said. "No need to decide this very second."

"Simone is right, you don't need to decide right now," Maddie said. "But please think about it."

* * *

Every lead Simone found on Trey went cold. Initially, Ralph was sure he spoke to Trey on the phone the day after Mohamed had dropped him off, as soon as he realized Mohamed and the BMW had gone missing. As he revisited the details in his mind, he began to question his memory and what had happened all those years ago. It was possible, he concluded, that he had left a message on Trey's voicemail and had not spoken to him after all.

It was also possible Trey had fled the country. Like his former boss, he had racked up a massive amount of debt. His outstanding bills were the result of a gambling addiction and several years of unpaid taxes. Unlike Mohamed, Trey was not beloved by family and friends. No one was looking for him. Almost no one Simone reached out to was willing to have a conversation. The exception was his stepsister. Even she had nothing good to say. Her theory was that Trey had squeezed every last cent from every relative gullible enough to be swindled and was living his best life in Paradise Island, Bahamas. It was one of the world's top poker destinations, and he'd boasted about an early retirement and sipping frozen rum drinks on the beach there.

It was more likely that Hazel's childhood memory told an appalling truth, that Trey had been killed for threatening to expose Don's crimes. It certainly tracked with Don's more recent misdeeds and the person he was revealing himself to be.

It was still dark outside when Maddie, Paula and Constance met at their usual spot for breakfast. On the agenda was planning their annual trip to Mexico. For the past few years, every January or February, the three of them escaped the Minnesota cold and vacationed together at a luxury resort in Isla Mujeres, off the coast of Cancun, where the Gulf of Mexico and the Caribbean Sea converge. For two weeks, they made it their mission to unplug and relax. Completely ignoring work emails and calls was not always feasible while they were away, but they managed to disconnect enough to enjoy the island's delicious food, luxurious spa treatments and warm white sand beaches.

"What about excursions?" Maddie asked, digging into a short stack of pancakes piled with strawberries and whipped cream. "Do we want to try something new this year?"

While they ate their breakfast, the women revisited memories of their previous activities. Twice they had taken golf cart tours around the island. They had almost always participated in daily sunrise yoga in picturesque Playa Norte. Their favorite excursion had been a visit to Punta Sur at the southern tip of the island, which was home to an ancient temple honoring the Mayan moon goddess. There they looked out from the steep, naturally carved cliffs toward Cancun and the bay. They shopped in the small Caribbean village and enjoyed lunch at a restaurant overlooking the Mayan ruin and sculpture garden.

"I'm proud of us," Maddie said. "For once, we are not talking about work."

Paula smiled knowingly as she pushed away her almost-empty plate.

"We always say we're going to swim with the dolphins—let's do it this year," Constance said.

"I'm up for anything that's not on a boat," Paula said. "Even the 30-minute ferry ride to the island makes me seasick."

"Speaking of boats, what were the DNA results from the items found in the McGuinns' boathouse?" Maddie asked. She spooned some of the whipped cream from her plate into her coffee and stirred.

"So much for no work talk," Paula scoffed.

Maddie conceded. "You know how much I hate being out of the loop."

"The clothing had been wet, but it had also been there for weeks," Constance said, and took a sip of coffee. "There have been cases where DNA was found on the clothing of victims several hours or even days after exposure to water. Unfortunately, in this case, any DNA that may have been on the items found in the boathouse was no longer present."

Outside the diner, snowflakes floated slowly to the ground and melted on the sidewalk. Maddie shifted her gaze toward the sky and thought of Hazel. "So no DNA to connect Don to his former father-in-law's homicide?" she said.

Constance took one more bite of her veggie and cheese omelet and wiped her mouth. "No DNA," she confirmed, folding the napkin and placing it on her plate.

"There is something else," Paula said quietly, looking directly at Maddie. "Addison left a note."

The waitress appeared, flipped through her pad and tore a green slip from it, which she placed on the edge of the table. "I'll leave this here, ladies," she said. "No rush and let me know if you need anything else."

"I've got this one," Constance said, handing over her credit card. "Thanks, Bonnie."

Bonnie took the card and headed toward the cash register.

"A suicide note?" Maddie asked.

"Yes," Paula said, reaching in her tote. "Among other things, it led us to this." She retrieved a document and handed it to Maddie.

It was a copy of a yellowed report stamped in red with the words "Marine and Earth Sciences Library, Oct. 3, 1973, N.A.O.O., U.S. Department of Commerce." It was titled "Great Lakes Ice Cover, Winter 1969-1970."

As Maddie flipped through the pages, she slowly realized what she was looking at. It was an official report detailing how thick the ice was on Lake Superior in Duluth some 40 years ago, at the time Don Koch, Addison and Brandon McGuinn, Frank Larson, Victor Price and William Parker—the high school hockey all-stars who called themselves the Cretin Six—had gathered on its shores. As she read, she fixated on the words:

"Early March 1970: Three large areas of open water were located along the north shore. One was along the southeastern shore of Isle Royale, and another at the entrance to Thunder Bay, extending westward to the vicinity of Grand Portage. The third area began just west of Grand Marais, Minnesota, and extended southwesterly to within a few miles of Duluth-Superior Harbor. This was the first time that so large an open water area has been observed in this end of the lake."

Mouth agape, Maddie looked at Paula and then Constance. Her sentences formed as she put the pieces together. "Frank Larson went back to Lake Superior while the others were sleeping to retrieve his boot from the frozen lake. But for the first time in recorded history, the lake wasn't frozen; there was open water. He couldn't see the open water in the dark—" Maddie dropped the report onto the table and covered her mouth with her hand.

Paula moved closer. "Don saw the open water in the light of day, when he returned to the lake to search for Frank. He convinced them all to lie for the sake of their hockey careers. It's a secret they've been keeping for decades."

Maddie felt as if she'd been zapped with a Taser. She took a drink of water and her words returned. "What else did Addison's note reveal?"

"We got him, Maddie," Paula said. "Don Koch is going away for a long, long time."

"Sorry to cut this short, friends," Constance said, checking her watch, "but I have to get going."

On her computer screen, Constance reviewed Charles "Chet" Hill's record in the Criminal Justice Information Services database. It included a mug shot of a young man with a sharp jawline, thick neck and stringy brown hair along with his criminal history. In 1978, he was caught shoplifting at a department store and charged with a misdemeanor. He was charged with a second misdemeanor for possession of cocaine later that same year. A few years after that, he held up a gas station at gunpoint and snagged more than $5,000 in cash. It led to a felony conviction and prison time.

Constance reviewed the notes on her desk. By all accounts, Chet had gotten his act together after court-mandated drug and alcohol treatment in 1985. He received an associate degree from Dakota County Technical College's automotive program. He took a job as a mechanic at Koch Automotive Group's Ford dealership in Vadnais Heights. In the years that followed, he hadn't gotten so much as a parking ticket.

FBI field agent James Jarvis appeared at the threshold of Constance's open office door. "Ready to go, boss?" he asked.

"Ready," Constance said. She tucked her notes into the folder and grabbed her jacket.

Less than an hour later, after Field Agent Jarvis finished setting up a tripod and video camera in Chet's living room, Constance began the interview. She sat on the sofa with her body angled toward Chet. He reclined sedately in a dingy brown tweed Lay-Z-Boy armchair dressed in baggy gray sweatpants and a worn-out sweatshirt. His face was gaunt, and his eyes and skin were jaundiced.

Constance announced the date, time, location and everyone in attendance. "Please state your full name for the record," she said.

"Charles John Hill," Chet said. His voice was heavy with phlegm.

"Mr. Hill, please explain why we are here today."

"I've got end stage pancreatic cancer," he said and coughed. "I wanna confess my crimes before I die." He struggled to clear his throat.

"And you are doing so voluntarily?" Constance asked.

"Yes, I am."

"Mr. Hill, do you understand that you can be arrested, even in your current medical condition, for the crimes to which you're about to confess?" Constance asked.

"Yes, I do," he said and took a jagged breath.

"What would you like to say?" Constance asked.

"I wanna say that I—" He coughed again and took a drink of water from the glass on the end table next to him. "I shot and killed Trey Calvers and Mohamed Assad and got rid of the bodies."

"Please start by telling us how you knew these men," Constance said.

"I didn't know Mohamed Assad. I knew Trey Calvers. We worked together. He was in charge of operations for the Koch Automotive Group dealerships and oversaw the service department. I had a felony on my record, but Trey hired me as a mechanic anyway. He said everyone deserved a second chance. We were friendly but didn't see each other much. I reported to the service manager, kept my head down, worked my ass off.

"Then, out of the blue, Don Koch wanted to meet with me and talk about Trey. Don hardly ever talked to the shop monkeys. I was surprised he even knew my name. I went to his office, and he told me how much respect he had for auto mechanics, said his dad had been one. He was real chummy. Asked what I knew about Trey's gambling problem. I didn't know shit, and that's what I told him.

"A few weeks later, Trey was fired, and Don called me into his office again to ask if I knew why. I told him there were rumors Trey was stealing from the company, but I didn't know what to believe. All of a sudden, Don turned into a real asshole. He said he looked into my employment record. Trey had never mentioned he'd hired an ex-con. Don said for all he knew I was in cahoots with Trey. I said I wasn't mixed up in anything illegal. I had served my time and turned my life around. My record spoke for itself. I was never late, worked long days and weekends without complaints, never took a single sick day. Don asked whether my loyalty was to him or Trey. I said I wanted to keep my job, I had a wife and daughter to take care of. Don said I would need to prove my loyalty."

"Did he have a specific ask?" Constance said.

"Not that day, but a few weeks later he invited me to his house in Minnetonka. He talked about a golf course development deal in Duluth that he was in on. The general contractor, Philip Lane, had been killed in a car accident. Trey threatened to pin it on him, tell the police it was no accident if Don didn't give him money."

Chet took a deep breath and choked. He clutched his abdomen and bent forward in the chair.

"Are you all right, Mr. Hill?" Constance asked. She leaned toward him and placed a hand on his shoulder. "Is there something we can do for you?"

"Where's my daughter?" Chet asked, his breathing labored.

"We asked her to wait in the kitchen while we conduct the interview," Constance said.

A mousy-haired woman appeared beside Chet's chair. "I'm here," she said and angled toward him.

"I need—" Chet said and sucked in a breath. "I need something for the pain."

"OK, Dad," she said and squeezed his hand. She turned to Constance. "He hasn't taken painkillers since yesterday. He wanted to be lucid for the interview."

Constance nodded. "Mr. Hill, are you OK to continue?"

"Yes," he said and sat back in the chair and took a deep

breath. "Trey threatened to go to the police about Philip Lane. Don wanted Trey dead. He said if I didn't do it, he'd have someone else kill Trey. And then he'd have them kill me and my family, too."

Chet's daughter reappeared and handed him two white pills, which he placed on his tongue and swallowed with a long gulp of water. She rubbed his back briefly and returned to the kitchen.

"Do you have proof Don asked you to kill Trey Calvers?" Constance said.

The corners of Chet's mouth slanted down. "I'm certain his daughter heard us talking about it. She was about the same age as my girl at the time. It probably scarred her for life."

"Why do you think that?" Constance asked.

"We were outside, on the back deck, and Don was ranting about putting a bullet in Trey's head," Chet said. He looked down at his hands, which were in his lap. "She was playing in the yard."

"Mr. Hill, please tell us about Trey Calvers' murder," Constance said.

His eyes were remorseful as he returned her gaze. "Me and Trey were on good terms. Don knew that. He wanted me to invite Trey to go to Mystic Lake Casino. Trey was all for it. I was gonna drive but when I got to Trey's place to pick him up, his driver, Mohamed Assad, was there. Trey was hell-bent on having Mohamed drive us so we could party.

"We got to the casino and ate at the restaurant. I had a beer, Trey had quite a few drinks. We played roulette for a while and then poker. Trey kept drinking and spending money like it grew on trees. I called Don at one point and said it wasn't going to work out, that Trey's driver was with us. He flipped out, said I needed to get it over with, kill both Trey and Mohamed. He told me to get Trey wasted and ask his driver to take me home, say I was too drunk to drive myself. He described a large plot of land in Woodbury that was no longer being farmed. He gave me directions to the land to give to Mohamed. He wanted me to tell him it was where my—" Chet's voice cracked, and he squeezed his eyelids shut. For several seconds, he said nothing.

Agent Jarvis stepped to the side of the video camera and cocked his head.

Constance watched Chet's chest rise and fall erratically. "Mr. Hill?" she finally said.

Chet opened his eyes and continued relaying the details:

On the drive from the casino back to the Twin Cities, Trey passed out next to Chet in the back seat of the BMW. As they approached the farmland in Woodbury, Chet asked Mohamed to pull over on the gravel road so he could relieve himself. The car rolled to a stop, and Chet removed a 9 mm pistol from his jacket pocket. He pressed the muzzle to the driver's head, forced him out of the car and several yards into the field. He shot Mohamed in the back of the skull and buried him in a shallow grave.

The realization of what he'd done and the thought of killing a second person—a man he knew—made Chet physically ill. His entire body shook, and he threw up the contents of his stomach. He stared at Trey's figure, still slumped over and inebriated in the back seat of the sedan and considered what to do next. The flash of headlights in the distance sent his thoughts into a tailspin. He couldn't go back to prison. Panicked, he stuffed Trey into the trunk of the car and shot him in the head. He slammed the trunk shut, got in the car and drove.

When Chet pulled into a 7-Eleven in St. Paul a half hour later, he could hardly recall how he'd gotten there. He called Don from the pay phone and sobbed. Don urged him to get his shit together unless he wanted to get caught and locked up for life. The convenience store he was calling from was near Loeb Lake, Don said, and he instructed Chet to ditch the car and Trey's body there.

Chet's responses became inaudible as Constance asked clarifying questions. Finally, exhausted from his efforts to come clean, Chet slumped in his chair. Constance got up from the sofa and nodded toward Agent Jarvis. He turned off the camera and began to pack up the equipment.

"Thank you, Mr. Hill," Constance said. "Your testimony will help us put Don Koch behind bars for the rest of his life."

* * *

The early December temperatures had not dipped low enough for lakes and rivers to freeze over, which made it possible for law enforcement to locate the 2002 BMW. Initially, a rescue boat was deployed on Lake Loeb in St. Paul. But the small body of water was thick with vegetation, which made the search imprudent. The Ramsey County Sheriff's Office Water Patrol Unit was called in.

Bundled in a nylon parka, Constance stood back from the shore with two of her colleagues from the FBI. They watched as divers in wet suits worked like synchronized swimmers, plunging and bobbing, plunging and bobbing. They dove under the water and sprung up to the surface multiple times as they attached cables to the car and ensured the woven lines were correctly positioned.

Almost two hours later, an oversized tow truck pulled forward on the shore. A rusted BMW slowly emerged from the lake bed, water, muck and plant life spilling from the car's cracks and crevices. Liquid continued to drain from the vehicle as the agents popped the trunk with a crowbar revealing exactly what Addison McGuinn's note and Chet Hill said they would find: the body of Trey Calvers.

"**W**CCO News has learned that the prosecutor in Minnesota auto dealer Don Koch's criminal case has filed shocking new charges against Koch this morning. Angie Jones joins us from Loeb Lake at Marydale Park in St. Paul. Angie—"

"That's right Dan, there is evidence that connects Don Koch to two homicides," the reporter said, holding a black gloved hand against her ear and earpiece, which were covered almost entirely by a winter hat. A heavy knit scarf was wrapped around her neck. The bulky TV station microphone in her other hand amplified the sound of the blowing wind. Behind her, white caps formed on the lake and mature trees along the shoreline waved their bare branches toward the sky. "Earlier today, officials recovered a black BMW sedan from Loeb Lake with a badly decomposed body inside. The BMW was from a fleet of luxury vehicles owned by Choice Car Service and was reported missing in 2002 with its driver, Mohamed Assad. The body in the car was not the driver's. Assad's remains were discovered earlier this year in a vacant lot in Woodbury; his death was ruled a homicide. The Ramsey County Medical Examiner's

Office has now confirmed the body pulled from Loeb Lake was former Koch Automotive Group executive Trey Calvers, and his death was also ruled a homicide. The FBI released a statement today that indicated there is evidence that connects Koch to Calvers' homicide. Koch was charged and taken into custody this afternoon."

"Angie, what can you tell us about Trey Calvers and his role at Koch Automotive Group?" Dan asked.

"Calvers served as chief operations officer for several years and was allegedly Koch's right-hand man until his employment was terminated in 2002—allegedly for embezzling company funds. Koch had a policy that forbade current and former employees from fraternizing. None of the Koch Automotive Group employees we spoke with kept in touch with Calvers after he left the company. A relative of Calvers who said he was estranged from the family long before he began working for Koch presumed Calvers had left the country."

"Was there a connection between Calvers and Assad?" the anchorman asked.

"We spoke with Choice Car Service owner Ralph Finney, who told us Calvers was a regular customer, and the last passenger Assad transported before his disappearance 11 years ago. We asked Finney if Calvers had filed any complaints or if there had been any conflict between Calvers and Assad. He told us he wasn't aware of Calvers being unhappy with the service; he always requested Assad as his driver and the two were friendly. Based on the charges, it appears the dispute was between Koch and Calvers, and Assad was collateral damage."

CHAPTER FORTY-FOUR

"This is a shocking turn of events and heartbreaking news for the victims' families," Dan said. "What happens now?"

Angie shifted, planting her feet to brace herself against the gusting wind. "According to the prosecutor, U.S. Attorney Paula Milton, in addition to the previous charges related to his bankruptcy case, Koch will face multiple criminal charges, including first-degree murder conspiracy and involuntary manslaughter. At this point, the judge and prosecution believe he poses a significant flight risk. He has been remanded to police custody and will be detained at the Hennepin County Jail until his trial takes place. The maximum sentence is 20 years for conspiracy to commit first-degree murder, and 10 years for involuntary manslaughter. Based on the additional changes Koch is facing, if convicted, it's likely he will spend the rest of his life in prison."

A green envelope caught Maddie's eye in a bundle of otherwise bland white mail dropped off by the postal carrier. It was addressed to her and Simone. There was a return address handwritten in the corner, but no name appeared with it, and the location listed wasn't familiar to her.

She stepped into her law partner's office. "Special delivery," she said.

"That doesn't look like legal correspondence," Simone said, her brown eyes peering over her colorful reading glasses.

"It's addressed to both of us," Maddie said.

Simone accepted the envelope, leaned forward and reached for her letter opener. She deftly sliced the flap and removed the invitation. "It's—" she said, her voice almost a whisper. "Mohamed Assad's family is hosting a celebration in his honor." She handed the card to Maddie.

Once the investigation of Mohamed's death had concluded, the medical examiner released the remains to his adult children, who were responsible for determining what would become of the body.

After migrating to Canada and settling in America,

Mohamed raised his children to take pride in their Islamic traditions. They were strong in their faith and prayed daily. They believed their present life was a trial for the eternal life to come. They donated to members of the community in need. During the daylight hours of Ramadan, they fasted to renew their awareness of and gratitude for everything God provided. The year before Mohamed disappeared, he and his children—who had not been to the Middle East—made pilgrimage to Mecca. It was Mohamed's first time returning since he and his wife had migrated west. Memories of her and their life there long ago came flooding back. It had been an emotional journey for all of them. They cherished the time together.

Under different circumstances, Mohamed's body would have been washed and wrapped in cloth after his passing. A funeral would have taken place immediately. The family would have dressed in black throughout a mourning period. While the details surrounding Mohamed's death had been especially tragic, they would still observe as many traditions as possible.

To honor their father, Mohamed's family would hold a funeral procession to the Islamic cemetery for a burial. A prayer service would be held at the mosque where they worshipped. Afterward, the Assads would host a gathering of family and friends at the Minnesota Landscape Arboretum, where Mohamed often tended to the rose gardens as a volunteer.

Maddie read aloud the note written at the bottom of the card: "Dear Madelyn and Simone," she said, her voice cracking, "Our family would be honored if you would join us in celebration of our father."

Tears came to Maddie's eyes and Simone reflexively handed her a tissue. Maddie hadn't expected such a strong reaction. The aftereffects of finding Mohamed's remains had rooted themselves deep within her.

"We should attend," Simone said.

Maddie dabbed Kleenex at the tears streaming down her face.

Simone came around the desk and hugged her. "I think it might give you the closure you're longing for," she said.

* * *

As Maddie and Simone entered the visitor center at the arboretum, they inhaled the sweet scent of roses intermingled with the aroma of savory Persian food. Just inside, they were greeted by Mohamed's three adult children—his son, Idris, and two daughters, Asma and Zara—all in their 30s. After introductions and condolences, the family directed them to sit at one of the reserved round tables at the front of the room where Ralph Finney and a few other people were already seated.

On the way to their table, Maddie paused, noticing rows of long skirted tables along the parameter of the room. They were covered with hundreds—perhaps thousands—of beautiful white roses arranged in large vases, along with objects and images that represented Mohamed. A framed photo of him and his wife, Minoo, on the day of their wedding ceremony was displayed. Several photos featured the two of them as young parents with their infants. There were pictures of the children and their father celebrating various milestones, including their trip to Saudi Arabia. And photos of Mohamed with his students—those he'd taught as a mathematics professor in Canada, and the younger children he'd tutored in the U.S. Photo collages featured Mohamed surrounded by beautiful rose gardens. Maddie held back tears as she and Simone took their seats.

Mohamed's son, Idris, made his way to the front of the room and addressed the multitude of guests. "Thank you for being here in celebration of the life of our beloved father." He swallowed hard before he continued. "Most of you know, our family has lived with uncertainty for more than a decade. When our father was reported missing, law enforcement told us we should not expect to hear from him because he had likely committed a crime and fled the country; if he re-entered the U.S., he would be tried and punished. His employer, Mr. Finney, assured the police our father was not to blame for the company's missing vehicle. He insisted, as everyone who knew our father did, Mohamed Assad was a man of immense integrity, intelligence and compassion."

Maddie glanced in the direction of Mohamed's daughters, whose heads of dark wavy hair bobbed solemnly in unison.

"Receiving confirmation of our father's death was painful. But there is freedom in knowing the truth. We are grateful to the handful of people in law enforcement and the criminal justice system who did not presume our father was guilty, who treated him like a human being, and who continued to search for answers, even after all these years."

He looked directly at Maddie and Simone, gave a single nod, and continued. "Just as there is freedom in truth, there is freedom in forgiveness. We know our father would not want us to harbor any anger. We know he would want us to celebrate his achievements and the difference he made in the lives of others and the world. That is what we will do here today."

Mohamed's older daughter, Asma, traded places with her brother and spoke about both of their parents, and how they fled Iran due to the economic conditions and lack of political and social freedoms. They left family and friends and the life they knew behind in the hopes of pursuing careers in medicine and academia. They planned to start a family of their own and wanted to provide a better life for their children.

Shortly after they arrived in British Columbia, Minoo was accepted into a medical residency program. Mohamed took an associate professor position at a respected university. They continued to advance in their careers. Minoo became an esteemed emergency room physician. Mohamed was a beloved professor of mathematics, admired by students and colleagues alike for his warmth and quick wit. The couple had one, two and then three healthy children. They were realizing the life they had always envisioned.

Their world turned upside down when Minoo was diagnosed with triple-negative breast cancer. When she became too ill to work, and the hospital insisted she take leave, Mohamed also took a hiatus from his career to care for his wife and their young children. During quiet moments, he tended to a small garden he'd planted in the courtyard with Minoo's favorite creamy white rambling roses, Felicite et Perpetue. After she died, when Mohamed was ready to return to work, he learned one of his colleagues had moved into his previous role as the head of the math department at the university. He took it as a sign, a message from Minoo, that it was time for a rebirth, to start something new. He became a math tutor to school-aged children. He worked part-time as a chauffeur driver. He also became a member of the Vancouver Rose Society and began entering his blooms in its annual rose show. He felt closest to Minoo when he was in the garden. He was certain she had a hand in his prize-winning roses.

Maddie turned to look at the photos of Mohamed surrounded by gardens and the vases of puffy roses on the tables. A tear ran down her cheek.

Mohamed's younger daughter, Zara, took her place at the front of the room. She spoke of how her family made their way to the U.S. and settled in Minnesota. Mohamed worked as a driver for Choice Car Service and volunteered as a math tutor. Clients and students adored him. He joined the Minnesota Rose Society and volunteered at the Minnesota Landscape Arboretum, tending to the rose gardens during the warmer months, and staffing the visitor service desk at least once a week all year long.

"As you leave here today, please take three white roses in memory of our father," Zara said.

The Assad family then invited others to share stories about Mohamed. Many people who came forward were those he had worked with. Ralph gave a heartfelt speech that had the entire room laughing and crying happy tears. The conversations about Mohamed's positive spirit and zest for life continued afterward at the luncheon. They enjoyed halva flavored with rose water and saffron, barberry rice with chicken, and a variety of other Persian dishes. The sounds of Persian classical music filled the air.

Maddie felt a sense of peace she hadn't before. She glanced across the table at Mohamed's family. "Thank you for the opportunity to be here," she said, placing a hand on her heart.

"We are very sorry for your trauma, Ms. Cummins," Zara said. "But we are grateful it was you who found him."

"In some strange way, it was if it were meant to be," Asma added.

"We appreciate everything you did," Idris said.

Maddie inhaled deeply. "I wasn't the one who got your father's case reopened. The FBI and U.S. attorney's office made that happen."

"You're being modest," Simone said. "You most definitely had a hand in it."

Maddie's cheeks flushed as she looked at the Assads. "For me, learning about your father has been a great comfort. I have loved getting to know him, if only a little."

Maddie, Simone and Ralph all stood, thanked the family again and said their goodbyes. On their way out, they each took a cluster of roses.

In the parking lot, Ralph paused at his vehicle. "It has been a pleasure getting to know you both," he said, hugging Simone and then Maddie.

Maddie choked back tears. "Mr. Finney, your willingness to talk with Simone, and your openness in providing details about Mohamed, helped get a criminal convicted," she said.

Ralph took Maddie's hand and squeezed. "Mohamed deserved justice," he said.

"He certainly did," Simone agreed.

Maddie nodded emphatically as the three of them huddled closely in a circle. "Thanks in large part to you," she said, locking eyes with Ralph. "I am finally at peace."

18 MONTHS LATER

Rows of sparsely furnished jail cells were stacked several tiers high. On the upper levels, just outside the dirty white cinder block walls and heavy steel doors, walkways were flanked by pipe railings and floor-to-ceiling chain link fencing. The fence had been attached to the rail to prevent inmates from jumping or pushing others off the passageway to the cement floor below. It was added years after the maximum security facility had been built, following a gruesome riot in this cell block. Beyond the fencing, across the stark echo chamber hallway, a thick multistory wall was dotted with large square windows.

Don knew it was early morning. The rising sun filtered through the murky glass across the corridor and beamed through the slot in his cell door like a laser, impossible to escape. He didn't know what day it was; they all melded together. Occasionally he thought about how he once tracked the precise passage of time on his collection of state-of-the-art Rolexes, and how now he didn't own a single watch. He didn't really need one. The guards conducted head counts five times a day, and there were scheduled meals, work and exercise. He knew it was spring based on the changing seasons, and about a year and a half since he had been sentenced to life without the possibility of parole at Oak Park Heights prison near Bayport, Minnesota.

Despite his conviction and the mountain of evidence against him, Don continued to proclaim his innocence to anyone who would listen. He claimed that the men who were once part of his inner circle and had testified against him—Brandon McGuinn, William Parker, Victor Price—were all lying. They had twisted the truth to save themselves. He said he'd only done as his attorneys had advised to get out from under the hundreds of millions he owed creditors. He insisted he'd been betrayed by his own legal counsel, whom he accused of kowtowing to an aggressive bankruptcy trustee and an overly eager U.S. attorney trying to make a name for herself. He maintained he wasn't a killer.

"Inmate," barked a guard who appeared at the door out of nowhere. "You have visitors."

"My lawyer?" Don asked. Though his last legal representation had been a public defender he had contact with only once since he'd been in prison, he'd recently received a letter from his daughter Hazel, informing him she was now a practicing attorney. She mentioned a potential visit to discuss his case. Since the letter, Don had boasted to fellow inmates about how his daughter was working on his appeal.

The guard shrugged, held out a pair of handcuffs, and directed Don to raise his arms and turn. Sloth-like, he did as he was told, shuffling toward the door, swiveling to face the white porcelain sink and toilet, and the single unmade bunk suspended from the wall. He held his position as the guard cuffed him.

"My daughter is an attorney," Don said. "She's going to get me out of this place."

"Mm," the guard grunted and nudged the inmate toward the hallway.

This was Don's first trip to the visitors' area. The floor was covered in glossy linoleum and there were rows of tables with attached benches, the kind you'd find in a school cafeteria. Two women were seated at a table, one whom he recognized immediately, though she was turned to the side. Her silky light brown hair covered her face, fell past her shoulders and down the back of her neutral-colored suit. As Don entered the room, his oldest child turned toward him. For the first time in months, he thought he felt something akin to joy.

"My beautiful girl," he said, his perfectly straight capped teeth forming into a Cheshire grin.

It took a moment for him to identify the second woman, who wore a suit the color of butter. When it registered it was his third wife's divorce attorney, Madelyn Cummins, his smile melted, and blood rushed to his face. "What the hell is she doing here?" he asked Hazel.

The guard's large hand firmly gripped Don's upper arm. "Compose yourself, inmate."

Don collected himself and relaxed his shoulders.

"All good?" the guard asked.

"Fine," Don said.

The guard directed him to sit on the bench at the opposite side of the table. Don fixed his eyes on Hazel. He longed to see her smile and the dimple in her right cheek. He hadn't seen her in the flesh for more than a decade, but he spotted traces of the girl he adored—her faded freckles, sparkly eyes and long lashes behind her tortoiseshell glasses. He recognized the parts of her that had come from Lisa. She was smart, classy and well-poised like her mother. She possessed the same qualities that had drawn him to his first wife. Everything changed a couple of years into his marriage with Lisa. She had a way of making him feel low-class, less than, never good enough. He shook off the thought.

"Thank you for coming to discuss my case, sweetheart," Don said.

"Hazel," she insisted. "You lost the privilege of calling me sweetheart or honey or daughter."

"Ha-zel," Don said in a singsong voice. "Despite everything, I'm still your father."

Hazel took in the sight of the man in front of her dressed in an orange prison jumpsuit. He was much thinner than he'd been at his trial 18 months ago, but he appeared rested and healthy. "Looks like prison is treating you OK," she said.

"Some of the men here can't stand the rigid structure, but I've gotten used to it," Don said. "I suppose I have military schooling to thank for that."

"Are you suggesting Cretin High School prepared you for prison?" Hazel asked.

Don chortled. "I guess I am."

"That's ironic," Hazel said, briefly making eye contact with Maddie, who raised a brow.

Don had nearly forgotten about the woman sitting next to

his daughter. "You haven't mentioned why she's here," he said.

"Did you notice my letter was written on stationery from Cummins and Backstrom Law Office?" Hazel asked.

He hadn't noticed, and even if he had, the names would not have registered. He had been focused solely on the news that his daughter was an attorney and wanted to discuss his case.

"Ms. Cummins is my boss," she said.

"You work for her? She convinced Jayne to take my baby girl from me," Don said, his right eye twitching.

"Let me remind you, Mr. Koch, it was your ex-wife Jayne who proposed the settlement agreement," Maddie said calmly.

"As I understand it, you were more than willing to relinquish parental rights to Gabby in exchange for a hefty financial settlement," Hazel said.

"Sweetheart, I didn't—" Don began.

Hazel raised a hand and shook her head. "Never mind," she said. "That's not why we're here."

"Right," Don said. "You're here about my appeal."

"I never mentioned an appeal," Hazel said. She sat up tall and tucked a strand of hair behind her ear.

"Your letter said—"

"That I wanted to discuss your case," Hazel interrupted. She took a breath and continued. "At your trial, Chet Hill testified that he shot, killed and disposed of the bodies of both Trey Calvers and Mohamed Assad per your orders—"

"Chet Hill never worked for me," Don blurted. "He's a lowlife and a liar."

"Please stop talking and listen," Hazel said firmly. "There's something you need to know about Chet Hill." She took another deep breath. "For years, my life was impacted by the trauma I endured as a child."

"What are you talking about?" Don asked.

"Over the past couple of years, I worked with a professional who helped me unlock memories of abuse, so I could process what happened and heal," Hazel said.

"Abuse?" Don said.

"Yes," she said and locked her eyes on his. "By you."

"I never laid a hand on you," Don said, blinking, only slightly bothered by the allegation.

"You're familiar with emotional abuse?" Hazel said. "When one person subjects another to behaviors that result in psychological trauma and often result in conditions like anxiety and PTSD?"

"You were not abused," Don said. His increasing volume attracted the attention of the guard. "You and your sister had everything you needed—clothes, jewelry, cars. For Christ's sake, Hazel, you went to law school. Do you think your mother paid for that?"

"It is our mother who has given my sister and me a good life, not you," she said. "And she managed to do so even after you drained her trust fund to finance a mythical golf resort development in Duluth."

"You were a child," Don said. "You have no idea what you're talking about."

"I know all about your sordid history in Duluth," Hazel said. "But I came here to talk about Chet Hill."

"Chet Hill will get what's coming to him," Don said. "His testimony will be discredited when my case is appealed. He'll be the one behind bars."

"He won't," Hazel said.

"What are you talking about?" Don asked.

"The memory came to me so clearly, as if it had happened yesterday," Hazel said. "I was sitting under the back deck at our house in Minnetonka, playing with my dolls. You and Chet Hill were on the deck above me, talking. You were pacing. You were very, very angry about something Trey Calvers had done. You ordered Mr. Hill to find Mr. Calvers and put a bullet in his head."

"Ha!" Don scoffed. "You were a little girl with a vivid imagination. That's nothing but a story you created in your head. It is not evidence. It proves nothing."

"I was too young to recall Mr. Hill's name, but I remembered Trey Calvers and how you insisted I say hello and shake his hand every time I saw him. I was traumatized by the thought of my own father killing someone. I was terrified that Trey Calvers might come for me. For years, I blocked out the memories. But they all came flooding back. And as horrible as that tsunami of memories was, recovering them and helping the feds convict you was the best thing I ever did."

"What the hell are you saying?" Don said. A clump of hair broke free from his slicked-back silver mop and fell onto his creased forehead.

"What I'm saying, Don, is that my childhood memories helped law enforcement find Chet Hill. Mr. Hill corroborated my story. He then provided information and physical evidence that was verified by forensic science and connected you to multiple murders. None of it can be disputed," Hazel said.

"You worked with the FBI?" Don said, clenching his jaw. "My own daughter?"

"As an officer of the court, it's my duty," Hazel said.

"You were a confused kid, and you're still delusional. I am not a killer," Don insisted. "It will be proven when my case is appealed."

"Mr. Koch," Maddie interjected. "You were tried, convicted and sentenced for your involvement in the deaths of Trey Calvers, Mohamed Assad and Peter Dickrell. In the 18 months since your conviction, an ongoing investigation has revealed you were responsible for the deaths of at least two more people, starting when you were a minor."

"Frank Larson was one of your best friends," Hazel said. "What kind of a monster lies about the death of his friend to save his hockey career?"

"That was 40 years ago," Don said. "I didn't kill Frank. Are you saying I had something to do with his disappearance?"

"Yes," Hazel said. "You also had something to do with the death of Philip Lane, the general contractor on your golf resort development project 20 years ago."

"You're out of your mind," Don said, his voice a low growl. "No judge or jury would believe I had anything to do with those deaths."

"You won't be tried for the crimes law enforcement un-covered since your conviction," Maddie said. "But the information they found will keep you locked up for life."

CHAPTER FORTY-SIX

"Fuck you!" Don shouted at Maddie.

"This visit is over," the guard said. He yanked Don off the bench and several feet back from the table.

"I am not a killer! My case will be appealed!"

"No, Don," Hazel called as the guard pushed him toward the exit. "Your case will never be appealed. You are never getting out of here."

Don continued to scream obscenities beyond the glass of the visiting room. A second guard escorted the women to the front of the prison, where they collected their jackets and bags.

"I'm proud of you," Maddie said. She slipped into her jacket, reached inside her purse, and put on her sunglasses. "How does it feel?"

"Like a reckoning," Hazel said. She took a deep breath. As though the weight of the world had been lifted from her shoulders, she released a long sigh.

The prison doors slid open.

"Trauma has been a common denominator for us," Maddie said. She wrapped an arm around Hazel's shoulder and squeezed as they walked. "But it was our resilience that gave us strength to keep pushing forward and to discover the missing pieces that haunted us."

The two of them exited the building and never looked back.

ACKNOWLEDGMENTS

First and foremost, I would like to thank the hotel night manager and police officers who came to my aid after I experienced a life-changing episode of transient global amnesia (TGA) in August 2020. I used my real-life experience as the basis for the plot of "Missing Pieces" and Maddie's trauma.

According to the National Library of Medicine, TGA is acute onset anterograde (unable to form new memories) amnesia that is temporary and usually occurs in middle-aged and older individuals. It is often precipitated by particularly strenuous activity or high-stress events.

The death of a loved one, divorce and moving are among the most stressful life events. Though I'd experienced unexpected death and divorce before, selling a house and moving amid the early days of the COVID-19 pandemic proved to be far more anxiety-inducing for me.

The night before I was to move into my new home, I walked away from the area Marriott after requesting a cup of coffee at the front desk. As with Maddie, when the night manager returned, I was gone, having left my purse at the desk. She recognized a guest in mental distress and contacted area police.

Clad in pajamas and a robe, with a heavy case slung over my shoulder, I wandered through residential streets and vacant lots near the hotel for several hours. When a police officer stopped his SUV and called me by name, I was stunned. When I asked how he knew me, he explained that the hotel manager's training told her something was wrong. She contacted authorities, which may very well have saved my life.

Only when the officer said they were concerned I may have wandered into traffic on a nearby freeway did the fog over my brain begin to lift. Still, I was unaware of what had happened during the hours leading up to my TGA experience. I did not know where exactly I had been, that I had fallen multiple times, or that there were bruises and cuts all over my body. I was only just starting to realize I was filthy and smelled terrible.

Once back at the Marriott, the team of officers wanted to bring me to the hospital, which I should have done without question but did not. The realization that I had two closings to attend and movers coming in mere hours was now clear in my mind. I convinced the officers I was fine and returned to my room. As was the case with Maddie, when I looked in the mirror the first time, I was stunned by the battered face staring back at me.

I would also like to thank my friend Debra Tourek. In the book, Maddie is hospitalized overnight, which I learned is standard procedure with TGA. In my case, when Debra learned what happened the next day, she insisted on driving me to the emergency room. The ER physician immediately ordered a CT scan to look for bleeding on my brain. The fear of the unknown was terrifying. When I learned the CT results were normal, I had never felt such relief in my life. The doctor informed me that TGA had caused my memory loss. Having heard of the condition only once in a cheesy movie, and certain it was something only a writer of fiction could make up, I almost laughed.

The doctor described how the anxiety of new home construction, selling my former residence, and the unknowns about COVID had conspired to cause more strain than I could handle. I recovered in less than 12 hours. TGA is fleeting but can last up to 24 hours. The doctor provided other intriguing data: On average, the ER staff of this midsize hospital encounters a case of TGA every six weeks. As a general rule, patients don't recall what happened and never suffer TGA again.

Experiencing TGA was frightening. I never recalled where I'd been or what I'd done that summer night, but in the weeks after the experience, I had brief flashbacks of walking, falling or standing in a vacant field—all things Maddie incurs. The disturbing dreams I had in the ensuing weeks mirrored those of Maddie's as well. My therapist explained that mentally I had to work through my trauma. Since my episode, I have encountered people with their own TGA stories, some far worse than mine. My bruises healed, and I was otherwise unscathed. My TGA experience ended positively too, with an added bonus that the seeds for a fictional story were planted.

In the months that followed my TGA experience, those seeds sprouted into words, which budded into chapters and grew into a murder mystery. With the support of my publisher, Chris Olsen, we continued to nurture the story and finesse the plot points. We didn't always agree, but I learned valuable lessons. Several experts were engaged in the process, including members of law enforcement and the FBI, an emergency room physician, and a trauma-focused therapist—I am thankful to everyone who had a hand in ensuring the story was as accurate as possible.

My thanks to the rest of the team at Publish Her, including Joy Riggs and Anna Befort, who are masters of copy editing and proofreading; Kayla Franz, who created the perfect book cover; and Leslie Lagerstrom, who made my first "Missing Pieces" book event at the Twin Cities Book Festival a wonderful experience.

ABOUT THE AUTHOR

Kathryn Schleich is a multi-award-winning author, feminist and activist in the Minneapolis and St. Paul area of Minnesota. Her novel "Darkness and Grace," a domestic thriller based on true events, received a 2022 Independent Press Award. Her crime novel, "Salvation Station," was honored with a 2021 American Fiction Award and was a finalist for a 2021 National Indie Excellence Award. Kathryn's writing has also been featured in two anthologies and various online publications. Her essay "Finding Hope in No Man's Land" received an honorable mention in Writer's Digest's Short Story Contest in 2020. Text from her academic book, "Hollywood and Catholic Women: Virgins, Whores, Mothers and Other Images," which evolved from her master's thesis, has been featured in college religious studies programs. When she's not writing, Kathryn champions youth literacy and press rights, and volunteers in the education and arts communities. Friends, family, traveling, good food and wine are important aspects of her life.

For more information about Kathryn, and to read her latest works, visit www.kathrynschleich.com.

ABOUT PUBLISH HER

Publish Her is a female-founded independent publisher dedicated to elevating the words, writing and stories of women. We are passionate about amplifying the voices of women of color, women with disabilities and members of the LGBTQ+ community, and we aim to make publishing an attainable, exciting and collaborative process for all. To learn more, visit www.publishherpress.com.